# GOD ON THE ROCKS

ALSO BY

JANE GARDAM

Fiction

*A Long Way From Verona*
*The Summer After the Funeral*
*Bilgewater*
*Black Faces, White Faces*
*The Sidmouth Letters*
*The Pangs of Love and Other Stories*
*Crusoe's Daughter*
*Showing the Flag*
*The Queen of the Tambourine*
*Going Into a Dark House*
*Faith Fox*
*Missing the Midnight*
*The Flight of the Maidens*
*Old Filth*
*The People on Privilege Hill*
*The Man in the Wooden Hat*

For children

*Bridget and William*
*The Hollow Land*
*A Few Fair Days*

Non-fiction

*The Iron Coast*

Illustrated

*The Green Man*

Jane Gardam

# GOD ON THE ROCKS

Europa Editions
116 East 16th Street
New York, N.Y. 10003
www.europaeditions.com
info@europaeditions.com


First Publication 2010 by Europa Editions



Library of Congress Cataloging in Publication Data is available
ISBN 978-1-933372-76-1

Gardam, Jane
God on the Rocks

Book design by Emanuele Ragnisco
www.mekkanografici.com

Prepress by Plan.ed – Rome

Printed in Canada

# GOD ON THE ROCKS

For Paul Scott,
in grateful memory

# 1.

Because the baby had come, special attention had to be given to Margaret, who was eight. On Wednesdays therefore she was to go out with Lydia the maid for the whole afternoon. Wherever Lydia liked. So long as Margaret's mother knew of course where that was.

Lydia said, the first Wednesday, that she had thought of the train. Maybe to Eastkirk—and a nice walk about on the Front and down the woodland. Margaret's mother said that Eastkirk meant money and the sands were better here at home, but Lydia said that Margaret would like the woods.

Teacakes were thus buttered and twirled in a paper bag and Lydia and Margaret took a train to Saltbeach and changed on to the single track line to Eastkirk and went slowly, see-sawing from side to side in the dusty coach with blinds with buttoned ends and a stiff leather strap arched like a tongue on the carriage door. The material on the carriage seat was black with red birds and very coarse and hard. There were two pictures above each long narrow seat on either side of a blotchy mirror. One picture was usually of Bexhill and the other of Bournemouth. They were sleepy, comfortable, upper-class places, decidedly foreign. The train stopped once on the way to Eastkirk, and through the open window you could hear the sea faintly breathe, at long intervals, below the cliff for the single track line ran close to its edge. Gulls stood about the platform or skimmed low, level over the distant cliff edge and the stationmaster's fine geraniums.

Margaret loved Lydia—or at any rate she loved the look of Lydia, sleepy and sunny like the pictures, with a huge fizz of yellow hair. Lydia had on, this first Wednesday, a dress of royal blue sateen with little red and yellow flowers, a bolero to match, high-heeled shoes and shiny silk stockings the colour of very ripe corn. She smoked a cigarette and held it in her bright red lips. When she took it out the cigarette had a pattern of fine red lines fanning together at the end. Lydia's thighs were broad and heavy under the silk dress, soft and flattened out on the red and black seat.

The sun blazed through the carriage window—it was a remarkable summer—hot as Bexhill or Bible countries. Lydia jerked about with the blind, fixing it first in one little sneck and then another, finally pulling it right to the bottom and pressing the button into the little brass hole. But still the sun shone in from the other windows across her lap.

At Eastkirk they got out on to the quiet platform and walked to the ticket man, and the train stood still as if it would never move again. Then it gave a long, releasing sigh and slowly eased itself off, haunch by haunch, towards Cullorcoates for Whitley Bay.

Margaret was a quiet child and Lydia was a quiet woman and they took hands and walked to the promenade without a word. It was summer holidays and young men stood about in clusters eating ices. Lydia and Margaret sat on a green seat high above the sea. Little ships bobbed. The pier was merry.

'Oi-oi,' said one boy. Lydia paid no attention but bought ices.

'What's oi-oi?' asked Margaret.

Lydia licked.

'Oi-oi, oi-oi,' said Margaret, wagging her legs from the knee down as she sat on the seat, liking her white ankle-socks and buttoned shoes. Other children ran about in sandals and shorts, but Margaret was neat with a hair-slide low by her ear and a cotton dress with smocking along the back as well as the front. 'It's only by the back you can tell,' her mother always said. 'You can tell a nice child from the back!' Some gulf obtained between Margaret and children with undecorated backs.

They began to walk along the Front, Lydia easily rolling, rather like the train. She was watched a lot and Margaret watched her being watched. She looked up at the high bulk of Lydia. 'You're a real bobby-dazzler,' her mother had said faintly when Lydia had come downstairs dressed for the outing—gone the maid's coffee-coloured dress and cap and apron of cream muslin, the black shoes and stockings. Margaret felt wonderfully proud to be walking beside Lydia so stately and at ease.

When they got to the beginning of the woodland, however, Lydia began to loosen up a bit. The path was steep down to the wood where the stream ran in to the sea and Lydia's high shoes toppled. 'Eeeeh dear,' she said. 'Eeeeeh dearie me!' Margaret began to skip and prance in front. The wood grew darker and higher and the sun was far away above, only dappling the earth under the trees now and then. There were few people about until they came out on a terrace above an ornamental bandstand where men in uniform were playing very sweet music in a loud and carefree way. People sat around the bandstand in rows of deck chairs, some of them with newspapers over their heads to keep off the sun but mostly, both men and women, in hats. The men wore panamas like Margaret's school panama but without the elastic under the chin, the women in broad-ribboned fine straws if they were old, or brimless cloth thimbles if they were young. Lydia said that they would sit down too but Margaret said she would like to go on and Lydia said all right then, and they wandered on into the trees again until it grew quiet and the splendid music died away. Lydia tottered over a tree root and cried out, 'Eeeeh dear!' again, laughing.

'Take them off,' said Margaret.

'And ruin me stockins?'

'Take off your stockings.'

Lydia sat down in the dark wood heavily and slowly and took off the high-heeled shoes and then stretched and heaved up above her skirts to release the suspenders of her orange stockings; three to each leg, front and middle and back. She rolled down the stockings and wiggled her toes. She stuffed the stockings down the front of her sky-blue dress. 'Carry me shoes then,' she said, 'and gis an 'and up.' Margaret pulled and Lydia arose. After a bit she said, 'Eeeeeh dear, me corset. I wish I could tek off me corset.'

'Well, do,' said Margaret. 'You can see right along the path and there's no one in the trees.'

Lydia however was unsure and they walked on together a good way until they came to a wavery side-path down towards the stream. They took this—and the wood was now very dark for such a brilliance above it—and met no one. They came to a dry stream bed with a rustic bridge over it. There was a gate on the bridge at their side of the stream and on the gate a white wooden notice saying PRIVATE. Across the bridge the wood cleared into a green circle of grass with a huge spreading tree over it. The tree's roots were liked webbed fingers and there were black triangular caves between them.

'You could take off your corset and put it in the tree roots for a bit,' said Margaret.

'Git on,' laughed Lydia. She leaned on the rustic gate and looked at the soft grass and the graceful tree with the sun shining through its branches in splashes. 'In' it bonny?' she said.

'Come on,' said Margaret and pushed Lydia which pushed the gate which opened and they giggled again and crossed the bridge. While Lydia took off her corset she made Margaret stand behind the tree. 'All right now,' she called in a minute and Margaret came back and saw Lydia rolling up the huge, pig-pink bundle all slats and eyelet holes and laces.

'That's better,' said Lydia, tying the laces to hold the whole thing together. Margaret took the bundle and felt it while Lydia scratched with both hands at the small of her blue silk back and then round to the front over each hip. 'Shove it undert' tree.' She laughed again, putting her head back. 'It's huge,' said Margaret. It was also heavy and warm and very damp but she did not say so. She pushed the thing quickly into the tree.

'Lovely,' said Lydia lying down. 'Grand.'

'What shall we do now?'

'I'll do nowt. Not owt. I's sweatin'.'

'Can I climb the tree?'

'Don't get yer dress mucky.'

'I'll take it off.'

'No.'

'Why not?'

'T'd not to.'

'Well look at you!'

'I'm me own boss.' Lydia knew limits for Margaret.

'It's not fair. I'll just tuck it in my knickers then.'

'Aye, tuck it in thy knickers.'

Lydia's eyes were closing. A big round flower, Margaret thought, climbing the sycamore. A big pudding of a flower. A big pudding on a dish. A big sticky pudding, juicy like an apple pudding. Fat and hot and squidgy like an eiderdown-pudding, she thought looking down at uncorseted outspread Lydia. Think I'll jump on her. Squelch and squish.

But at the top of the tree she shot her head out into the bright air. There was a breeze. The thinner branches swayed, the plates of pointed leaves were finer up here and greener. The faint sound of the faraway band blew up. The tree-top swung.

Margaret wanted to laugh and weep. She took the two topmost branches in her hands like the reins of a horse or a water-diviner and with her head still collared by leaves she sang very noisily a song about a baby falling falling falling down. Down and dead, dead and down, on his head, baby dead, until her own head was burning hot and a foot in the buttoned shoe slipped a bit and she went into watery terror and began to feel with her feet downwards, downwards till the branches thickened to comforting bars, then to elephant legs and then—with a thump as she landed on the circle of grass—were not important.

'I've been to the top,' she cried, 'I've been *over* the top.' She felt the silky boiling crown of her head again and looked round for Lydia. But Lydia was not there.

'Lydia?' she called.

'Lydia?'

There was almost complete silence in the wood. There was the dry stream bed, the rustic bridge, the flattened, sun-splashed grass where Lydia had lain. Quickly Margaret looked in the tree-root for the corset which was there.

But Lydia was not there.

'She'll be in the bushes,' Margaret thought. 'Lydia!'

There were some crackles and rustles of perhaps field mice or frogs, but no Lydia. Margaret went over and stood on the bridge and kicked at it a bit with her round-ended shoes. She climbed on the rustic logs of its cross-over rustic side and hung over. Then she slithered down the bridge from below. Then she squished about in the pale mud which was the stream and looked around at one thing and another.

'Lydia,' she called more sharply when she had scrabbled her way up the bank again, 'Lydia?'

A short distance behind the green, lawn-like pool of grass beneath the tree was a bank of other trees, very steep and thinning to sunlight along a ridge, and Margaret began in a great hurry to rush up this bank. 'Lydia,' she shouted now. 'Where are you, Lydia?' At the top of the bank fear suddenly had hold of her and made her hands heavy and her legs wobble. Tears came in to her eyes. *'Lydia!'*

She shot out of the trees at the top of the slope into wide empty sunshine. There was complete silence, not a soul about, just a great swelling plain of upward-curved parkland sleeping in the afternoon. Several immense trees stood about on it, dark gold and as still as cut-outs. Beyond them, far away, stood a massive yellow house. Its eyes watched her. She stared back.

Then below she heard quite a long way off Lydia calling Margaret.

'Margaret? Where you gone? I lost yer.'

She turned and flew down the bank. Lydia stood on the far side of the bridge.

'I lost you,' shouted Margaret, 'I lost you. I hate you.'

'I was just int' bushes,' said Lydia. 'It's time we went home. I was washing me hands int' bushes.'

'Why didn't you go this side in the bushes?'

'I didn't like.'

'I was lost.'

'You'd not of got far,' said Lydia.

After she had got into the corset again they ate the teacakes out of the paper-bag and walked up through the wood and passed the band. In the train Lydia said, 'Wherever did yer tek off til, anyway?'

'Nowhere,' said Margaret. 'If I tuck my dress in my knickers can I get in the rack?'

Lying in the luggage rack above Lydia, rocking like a sailor, she said, 'Can we go there again next week?'

'I'm not bothered,' said Lydia. 'If yer want.'

## 2.

Mrs Marsh, Margaret's mother, was a great breast-feeder at a time when it was fashionable to be otherwise. Nor had she shingled her hair nor seen to her waistline. She was a largish, loose-jointed, still-young woman much given to God and sympathy and immensely loving to babies. She sat hour after hour in her bedroom, knees apart in a nicely-made but antique sort of a skirt, deeply-waved brown hair falling round her face untidily.

Sometimes she had flour on her face, for she seldom looked in the glass and was fond of cooking. As she fed the baby she looked into its face all the time with a very gentle deep expression. When Margaret came into the room she would raise her head with a long and understanding look.

'Going out, dear?'

'No.'

'I thought it was Wednesday.'

'It is. That's this afternoon.'

'What, dear?'

'Going out.'

Mrs Marsh, dazed about times of day, detached herself from the baby, drawing herself back and mopping about with a cloth. She lifted the baby up on her shoulder where a huge towelling nappy lay, hanging a little way down her back for the baby to be sick on. She massaged its back, which was like the back of a duck, oven-ready. The baby's unsteady head and swivelling eyes rolled on her shoulder, its round mouth slightly open, wet and red. It seemed, filmily, to be trying to take in Margaret, who was fiddling with things on the mantelpiece behind her mother. She looked down at it with a realistic glare. The baby under the massage let air come out of its mouth in a long explosion and pale milk ran out and over its chin.

'Filthy,' said Margaret.

'There's my little lovekin,' said Mrs Marsh. She lifted the baby into the air before her, both hands under the armpits, and let it hang like dough about to drop. 'What did you say, dear? It's your treat-day with Lydia, isn't it?'

'This afternoon,' said Margaret, dropping the baby's bottle of gripe water and smashing it to bits on the mottled cream tiles of the fireplace. Glass flew everywhere in splinters, and the baby, after jerking as if it had received an electric shock, began to cry like a new lamb. 'Lair, lair, lair,' it went, scarlet in the face and flushing quickly to purple all over its bald head, its eyes in two directions.

Mrs Marsh was not upset, though she had jumped as violently as her son. Margaret saw her take the decision to be understanding rather than annoyed. 'There now,' she said. Placing the lamenting child over her other, nappiless, shoulder she drew Margaret to her to lean upon the other one. 'Never mind, dear. Just an accident.'

Margaret—her mother smelled of milk and baby powder—pulled away and made a face. 'It's like a pig,' she said.

Mrs Marsh looked yet more understanding.

'Darling, you do know how much we love you, don't you? He's your baby too, you know, just as much as ours. Look—you hold him. You're such a big girl. He's going to love you so much.'

'What's so marvellous?'

'Marvellous?'

'About that? Why do I have to be pleased that he's going to love me? I don't need him.'

'*He* will need *you*.'

'No, he won't. If I wasn't here he wouldn't know anything about me.'

'But you are here.'

'I'm not here for him. I managed without me. Nobody was here for me when I was born and I was all right.'

Mrs Marsh, trying slowly to digest this empirical point, wrapped the child very tight in a cloth with its arms crossed over its chest tight beneath it, then put it on its face in the flounced organdy of the crib.

It did not look up to its surroundings. More like a trussed duck than ever.

'It can't be good for it, bound up like that,' said Margaret, and Mrs Marsh brightened at a sign of possible concern. 'Oh yes it is, dear. It says so in Truby King. They like to feel safe.'

'I don't see why you feel safe if you're tied up.'

'Not tied up, dear. Just well wrapped round. Babies come from a very warm place,' she said, coy but emancipated. 'Safe in a little nest in their mummies' tummies.'

'I wouldn't say a *little* nest,' said Margaret. 'It was huge. And all rippling about. You could see it even, at the end. When some of the Saints came in just before that Sunday I was nearly sick. You ought to have been ashamed. All huge.'

'Now why ashamed?' asked Mrs Marsh, very bright. She had secretly found some Freud to read in the Public Library during pregnancy, as well as Truby King. 'Now why ashamed? It's quite natural. After all, it's how we all came, darling.'

'Pity we did.'

'Now, Margaret, how silly.'

'It would be better without people.'

'There would be no love, darling, without people. God made us so that there might be love. Er—one John four—er—twelve, isn't it? No—John one fourteen—but . . . '

'Why bother? The world was all right before, it seems to

me. If we didn't exist we weren't missing things. Ice and fire and snow and glaciers and then plants. It would have been enough you'd think. Well perhaps dinosaurs. If I'd been God I'd have left it at dinosaurs. I'd have been satisfied looking down at all that.'

Mrs Marsh said very carefully, 'Margaret, I don't think you ought to talk about dinosaurs. You know what Father thinks. I suppose this is school.'

'No. It's just real. They've found the bones. Father doesn't underst . . . '

'Of course Father knows there were dinosaurs. But you know that we believe in Genesis here, don't you? You've known this for a long time. You especially, Margaret, with your wonderful memory. Most people nowadays don't, they believe in a very old-fashioned idea that was disproved years ago by people your father knows all about. Most people believe in *myths*—you know what myths are?—invented by Sir Charles Darwin about how we grew out of fishes and monkeys and things. Doesn't that seem silly? But in this house we believe that God put us down all complete, Adam and Eve in the garden, so that we could share all the lovely things God had made.'

'Very kind,' said Margaret, 'but . . . '

'Exactly!' Mrs Marsh looked really delighted now whereas, considering dinosaurs, she had seemed uncertain. 'Exactly. Kind.'

'Unnecessary,' said Margaret. 'God and the world would have done. Like me before the baby came.'

'Now, Margaret dear, I know you don't realise it but that is blasphemy.'

'What's blasphemy?'

'But you hear about blasphemy every week at the Primal Hall!'

'Is it what Father talks? I thought what Father talked . . . '

'Margaret! Blasphemy is taking the name of God in vain.'

'In vain. A lot of things are in vain.'

'No. It means lightly. You are taking the name of God lightly.'

'Better than heavily.'

'God,' said Mrs Marsh going rather red in the cheeks and buttoning her dress after adjusting a massive camisole beneath and easing herself to an even balance, 'made us in his own image.' She looked at the trussed baby, face down, its red head like a tilted orange rearing up and down on the undersheet as if desperately attempting to escape. Giving up, it let its head drop into suffocation position and there was another explosion followed by a long, liquid spluttering from further down the cot: and a smell. 'Oh dear,' said Mrs Marsh contented, 'now I'll have to start all over again with a new nappy. Could you hand me the bucket, darling?'

'His own image,' said Margaret watching the horrible unwrapping. 'If God looks like us . . . What's the point?'

'You must speak,' said Mrs Marsh sternly, 'to your father.'

# 3.

They walked to the ice creams, but unlike the previous Wednesday did not sit on the seat overlooking the sea. They licked the ices as they walked along, passing the oi-ois and the whistles, to the turnstile to the wood, and slowly—for it was an even hotter day than last week—they set off down the woodland path. Lydia said she'd somehow last till the bandstand before taking off her shoes and when they got to the terrace above it they sat down on the grass, finished the ices, and looked down. Flower-beds surrounded the bandstand lawn in the shapes of hearts and diamonds as if big biscuit cutters had bitten into the grass. Inside each shape was a pattern of artificial-looking plants, first a diamond or a heart of leathery clumps the colour of purple cabbages, then a round of succulent yellow-green, then a blue lobelia and, in the centre, a triumph of vermilion geraniums. Between the beds and the bandstand was a circle of green and white deck chairs. In the bandstand the band played, very confident and strong.

'Let's go down,' said Lydia and they went and sat in two deck chairs, buying penny tickets. Lydia lay back watching the bandsmen who became aware of her.

After a bit she said to Margaret, 'D'yer want to 'ave a laff?' and took out of this week's paper bag an orange which she peeled, throwing the peel at her feet. She parted the pieces of orange, and slowly slid them into her mouth, watching one particular bandsman all the time. In a moment water came out of his trombone in a spray. Margaret found she was laughing out loud and Lydia gave her a nudge and silently doubled up in the chair. 'We used to do it in Bishop,' she said, 'when I were a lass. At all t'processions.'

'Are there a lot of processions in Bishop?'

'Oh aye. Watch again now.' She fastened her attention on another player, a tuba player who was very damp in the face and robust rosy red. The collar of his stiff blue serge uniform looked like a throttle. His very eyes were hot, and bulged from between the eyelids like brooches. His expression was anxious. 'Wait on,' whispered Lydia and sucked the orange.

Out flew the spit and a strange dark note broke into the melody, making the conductor, whose back was of course to the audience, turn to the tuba player with very vigorous arms. Margaret and Lydia collapsed against each other in not quite silent laughter, tipping their chairs, and an official came up and asked them to leave.

'We've paid tuppence,' said Lydia with streaming eyes. Shushing came from the surrounding chairs, newspapers were taken from heads. Panamas turned. 'There's no rule agen eatin' oranges, is there?' She was enjoying herself.

'There is against litter,' said the man, pointing at the peel.

Lydia picked it up and pressed it all in his hand. 'Sorry,' she said, lifting her shoulder and dropping her eyelids, which were shiny with Vaseline. She smiled up at the man and closed her teeth over another piece of orange. 'You get off now,' said the man in a fluster. 'I'm comfy,' said Lydia, stretching out and crossing her feet. Margaret said, 'Let's go, Lydia.'

'No. I'm resting me feet. We've paid tuppence.'

'Do let's go.'

'Okay then,' said Lydia, ever pliant. 'Bye, beautiful. 'Elp us up.' The official looked stern and glared about him as he gave his arm. Lydia turned to the tuba player and winked, and there followed two very unfortunate mistakes in the phrase he was engaged upon as the two of them went hand in hand up into the wood.

At the private bridge they stopped a moment and Lydia said that now she'd take off her corset and rest and they pushed open the gate thankfully as if they were going home.

'I'll climb the tree again,' said Margaret.

'Don't kill thysen.'

'Don't disappear.'

She climbed higher and higher. Near the top she stopped to see whether she might not be able to take a different direction so that at the very top she would be able to look over at the house, but there seemed to be no obvious route. She tried a rather spindly fork that grew to a good height and over in the direction of the bank she had climbed when she was looking for Lydia, but when her head came out at last all she saw were the trees of the bank itself which was still a little higher than the high sycamore. There was still a barrier; only over her shoulder could she see the tree-top carpet that stretched along above the stream over towards the bandstand and the sea, and the sky overhead. Her foot slid and she slipped down the tree, crackling through the slim branches, luckily landing in a safe cleft below. From away down on the ground she heard Lydia shout and then another voice, a man's. 'I'm all right. Don't fuss,' she called, but sat on, riding the tree, getting her breath back, examining for some time the long lavender and white graze on her arm, watching it turn to blebs of scarlet and then begin to bleed quite creditably. 'I'm bleeding a bit. I'm all right,' she called down again as there was silence. She felt undervalued when there was no reply.

Lydia was on the bridge resting a hip against the rail, and smiling and leaning over the little gate facing her was a man who was smiling too. He was in a dark cheap suit but looked an out of doors man. He had a hungry, ageing indoor face but rough hands. He appeared to hold some sort of authority in the place but was smiling slyly as he exerted it. Margaret felt these contradictions, and distaste.

'Lydia!'

Lydia did not turn but tossed her head back, looking at the man. 'You can't stay here, you know,' he said. 'I saw you last week.'

'Why not?' Lydia asked. She watched the man closely, looking at him all over as if he were more interesting to her than his answer.

'Can't you read?' He came through the gate and tapped the board on the outside of it. 'Private.' Margaret dropped out of the tree with a thud but neither of them turned round.

'I'm bleeding,' she called.

'Oh git on,' said Lydia, looking down at her blackcherry finger nails, and leaned farther back against the bridge. Margaret hoped it was safe. Lydia's great back, without the corsets, looked very powerful. She was in the blue sateen again. Her legs beneath it were like long thick bottles. Her feet were broad and each big toe was yellowish and square. Yet she looked very lovely somehow. 'Git on,' she said to the man. 'It's bonny 'ere. Why not?'

'It's private property.'

'Lydia!'

Still they paid no attention. 'Is she your sister?' the man asked, not taking his eyes off Lydia.

'No. I'm the maid. I tek her out.'

'Cushy, eh?'

'It's since the baby. It's the holidays. Gives the mother a rest. There's not much else to do of an afternoon anyway.'

'It's your afternoon off then?'

'Not likely. I'm not *that* daft.'

'When's your afternoon off?'

'That's my business.' But she laughed and heaved herself off the bridge rail and walked before him towards the tree and Margaret, slowly. She was twirling a leaf.

'Good place then, is it?'

'Not bad.' She took notice of Margaret at last. 'You goin' int' stream?'

'No. I'm bleeding. I fell down the tree.'

'Keep you at it, do they? Cook-general, are you?'

'No. I'm just general. She cooks.'

'She cooks, eh? Not class then?'

Lydia lay down on her side under the tree like a range of quiet hills. 'Git on now, Margaret,' she said. 'Don't just stand there. Gis a look a' yer arm.'

'You not in a class place then?' said he.

'It's not owt,' said Lydia stroking the graze. 'Come 'ere. I'll kiss it better.' She pulled Margaret's arm down and kissed the inside of it slowly. Margaret drew her arm back quickly and scrubbed at it with her hand. 'You don't have to *kiss* it,' she said. The man took out a packet of Goldflake cigarettes and offered one to Lydia and lit it and one for himself. 'Don't you like her kissing you?' he said—still not taking his eyes from Lydia. Margaret did not reply but went a little way up the bank behind the tree towards the sun at the top, and the house. 'Here. You come back,' said the man. 'Where are you going?'

'I'm going for a walk.'

'You can't go up there,' said the man. 'I've told you. It's private.'

'What is it then?' asked Lydia. 'Some park or somethin'?'

'That's it,' he said. Turning to Margaret who was standing now quite far up the bank he said, 'Do you hear me? Come back down.'

'Come on down,' said Lydia.

They turned back towards each other—the man sitting on a log smoking the cigarette with quick sharp puffs, Lydia sleepily watching the smoke rise up from hers in the rays of the sun slanting through the sycamore. 'Int' smoke bonny?' she said. 'Look at it. It's like a lovely scarf.'

Margaret sat down among the trees on the bank. 'Can I go on up, Lydia?' Neither of them answered her. The man said, 'What you called?'

'Lydia,' said Lydia, watching the smoke.

'I'm going on up,' shouted Margaret, but there was no reply and she went on up and when they were quite a long way below her she turned and shouted again, 'I'm going then. I'm going on up. Even if it is private.'

The figures were very still under the tree and did not turn. As she reached the great grassland and the sunshine she heard Lydia's sleepy long laugh.

There stood the house again with the parkland in front of it and the huge spaced-out trees. It was a bright sandy house and the grass, all the wide swell of it, in the height of this astonishing summer, was dried sand-yellow too. The huge trees were a bright but darker yellow, surprised by autumn before their time. Their leaves already looked shrunken and curly under the sky of clear, steady blue. Under one of the trees a man was sitting at an easel painting. He had a large stomach under a good white linen jacket and wore a cream-coloured straw hat. He touched the canvas with the tip of a long brush and Margaret could see beneath the hat-brim a golden beard. All was yellow, white, cream and gold against blue, and the light was like a song. Margaret shot back into the trees.

The man however did not move and had obviously not noticed her, so she took off her shoes and socks and began to walk along just inside the trees until she was behind him but much farther away. She looked over at his squat back now and saw the view that he saw and was painting though she was much further away from it. It was the house, the huge flank of it bare of windows, just a vast surface of sandstone with the bastion of the chimney flues giving angles of shadow and a spidery creeper netting part of the lower half with brilliant papery red leaves. Margaret thought it was an odd thing to paint the house where it had no windows. The man must be silly—just trying to be clever. But he looked very sure of himself somehow. Very solid and engrossed.

She came to a brick wall with an iron door in it and looked in at a huge high-walled kitchen-garden with several broken greenhouses. A lot of the vegetable beds were bare from the drought. Outdoor tomatoes were rows of shrivelled leaves, the fruit bulging in among them blackish red. Margaret went in and took one off its frizzled stem and ate it. It was splitting and the split had a rough dark frilly edge like a nasty cut. Some of the other tomatoes had fluffy stuff on them and there were gnats about. Margaret's mother had been going on about what a terrible year it had been for tomatoes. 'And scarcely a bean.'

That was true too. The bean bed here was a show. A few scrawny yellow things hung down among the rows of wires and brittle stalks. They had not been watered. They were much worse than the beans at home in the back-yard. Margaret's mother and even father, Margaret and Lydia had been taking the washing-up water to the beans—every drop—for weeks. The gardener here must be very lazy.

Margaret suddenly knew that the gardener would be the man who was talking to Lydia.

She turned a corner then and walked on to a pink brick path with cutting-flowers down each side of it—lupins and red-hot pokers and gladioli but all very poor and dry. It was so hot here that the sun seemed to beat with a pulse on the bricks. Black seed pods lay split wide open on stalks. A little oily water in the middle of what was meant to be a pond held the shadows of a cluster of muddy goldfish. Lily roots writhed shamefully in the open. A black wooden toy windmill on a stick meant for a scare-the-birds was warped and immovable. It was a garden neglected for much longer than one summer.

At the end of the brick path a nurse was sitting on a bench knitting under some huge exhausted sunflowers. Like the painter she sat determinedly as if she would be here for a long time, and Margaret, as the nurse released a length of white wool out of a bag, raising her navy blue arm high in the air and briefly looking up, had just time to step out of sight behind a shed.

And then she saw what it seemed she had known she would find and the horror of it was like remembered horror and yet a terrifying shock. Under the garden wall in what little shadow there was, at some distance from the nurse and at an angle from her, was a long high box on spindly wheels.

It was a basket-work box, wider at one end than the other and as long as a grown person. It had black wavy wires at the narrow end and a bar to push it along. Inside you could see that it was padded in some way. It was a monstrous, shallow pram.

Margaret knew she must look in the pram. She stood some way from it. Behind the shed was the remains of a bad bonfire—white ash, the odd blackened tin, lumpy rubbish. Beyond this was a cinder path to a back gate. Looking all round Margaret saw nobody. The nurse was out of sight, round the corner of the shed. All was quiet, safe, utterly still. She walked forward clutching her shoes with her socks stuffed one in each and peered over the cot side.

Lying in the shallow trough was a woman staring at the sky. She was thin as sticks with a little brown head like wood, the head of a wooden little monkey. The hands were bundles of spotty twigs lying on a thin white sheet. The skin of the face and hands was very dark, as dark as an Indian's. Only her eyes were bright—blue and alive, liquid and huge they stared upwards. The rest of her under the sheet was only to be guessed at, so small it was nearly invisible. Apart from the head and the hands the pram might have been empty. The face looked like the face of the oldest creature in the world.

# 4.

The almost permanent pietà of Mrs Marsh and the baby was the only sensuous thing in the house. It was a house in a long, dark-red terrace facing the sea—a biggish house with big but ugly windows inside a narrow concrete trough and a low brick wall with short lumpy railings along the top. There was a heavy and decent front door and very clean, colourless curtains, the same in every window like a private hotel. The front room was never used except on Christmas afternoon. It was crowded with huge fawn armchairs with fawn cushions and a table in the window stood with a thick cream flower vase, dead centre, which had never held a flower. Beside the vase was a Bible which could be seen clearly from the road.

The house was what is called a good house. Marsh was a bank manager. He was moreover suspected of being if not rich, very comfortable, though there was not a hint of it in his conversation or appearance and very much the reverse in his activities. He and his wife were members of the Primal Saints and most of their free time was spent in the local Primal Hall down Turner Street—a very nasty street of plum and sandstone and silence. Twice on Sunday and one evening in the week Marsh's careful small face was raised to his God and the unlikely loudness of his prayers drowned any noise from the chip shop and the pub round the corner. Not an empty chip bag dared blow its scratchy way down Turner Street when Marsh was praying for those who preferred to lean on the railings eating the chips rather than contemplate eternity. Mrs Marsh and Margaret and the baby sat—Mrs Marsh placidly—watching him. Mrs Marsh sometimes cried out 'Alleluiah' or 'Praise the Lord' at intervals the Lord dictated, as professionally as anyone—as professionally as barmy and holy Bezeer-Iremonger, gassed and good, the old mystery who had been there since the end of the War.

Mrs Marsh was a convert. Her family had been vaguely C of E. She had accepted her husband's faith after a fervourless girlhood from a mixture of reasons badly thought out. Her mind anyway had been at the time on other matters, for it was Marsh's solemnity and interest in good that had first excited her—and Marsh so stern and steady and small at home had been such an astonishment in Turner Street. Genesis and Exodus and the prophets thundered in her ears and set up tingling of a different order from any which had threatened their untalkative courtship or their never-discussed and businesslike interludes in bed. The eyes of the Saints shone in Turner Street. They smiled at Mrs Marsh admiringly, enviously as she left the hall.

She loved Marsh. She loved him in fact on Sundays more than at any time they had ever been alone. Except for the first time. Had she known it she was like a wife standing by a husband at a football match watching a yelling stranger, deliciously excited to find she shared a bed with a man she hardly knew.

It was her only excitement.

For as a Primal Saint Mrs Marsh knew nothing of football matches, nor cinemas, nor theatres, nor concerts. She could address herself to no painting or graven image or new hat. She couldn't drink alcohol. She could eat—so long as it was not excessively or with delight, but she must never buy a cigarette, paint her face or improve on God's ideas for her hair. 'I am a convert,' she would often say calmly, knees apart, easy. Only in the smocking on Margaret's dresses and the flounces on the baby's cot was there sign of a regression, and Marsh spotting these and surprised that she could not see in them the whiff of sin had prayed sometimes about them. On his short straight-toed walk to the bank and back he sometimes wondered why smocking and flounces were the petty things from the world of the damned she held dear, and let remain. But remain they did.

And so did Lydia.

Before Lydia Mrs Marsh had done without a maid, and no great hardship. Though the house was big it was so bare and tidy it caused nobody much trouble. Marsh had a clean shirt every day which Mrs Marsh slowly and peacefully ironed each evening. His shoes seemed to stay polished and his suits never seemed to need pressing. The cooking he liked was plain, no hobbies sullied the household and the only book left about to gather dust was the front room Bible. Margaret was quiet and good and spent most of her time alone, school friends who were not Primal being discouraged.

And then, with the baby, Lydia was in their midst. There had been some sort of a muddle which Margaret and her mother never fathomed. Some distant Saints in Bishop Auckland had recommended a good girl wanting a place—from a devout family, strong in the faith and a good scrubber—and a week or so later, like a rainbow on the step, had stood Lydia drooping a cigarette and carrying a battered gladstone bag. Mrs Marsh had stood very still and Marsh turned quickly away to his room.

'Me trunk's ter foller,' Lydia had announced, striding in.

'I think,' said Mrs Marsh, 'you will have to take off your—lipstick.'

'Oke,' said Lydia lighting another cigarette. 'Shall I mek tea?'

Mrs Marsh flew to open the kitchen window. 'Oh—no smoking!' she said. 'Didn't you know—?'

'Oke,' said Lydia putting the cigarette out by dropping it in the sink and running the tap on it. 'Don't look so scared. I'll keep it to me room.'

'We thought—you see, we thought—,' she said. 'Didn't you know? Mr Marsh, and I of course, and the children—we are The Faithful.'

'Think nothing of it,' said Lydia. 'Where d'you keep yer butter?' She had begun to cut scones. Then she began to butter them thickly and put them on a plate. She had piled them up in a way that looked comforting and caught Margaret's eye as the kettle began to sing. 'Int' they bonny?' she asked. 'How about jam?'

Coming into the dining room to remove the empty plates later she had stood for a moment arms akimbo surveying the scene and then as if satisfied began to stack a tray up with dirty dishes. 'Pass up now, Margaret,' she had said as if she'd been there for years.

'Just a moment,' Marsh had looked at her. 'Shall we say Grace?'

When she had left the room he had sat staring in front of him.

'Of course,' said Elinor Marsh humbly, 'I know. She will have to go.'

'Why?' He lifted neat brows.

'Well, I thought you'd . . . I mean the henna and . . . '

'She has been sent,' said Marsh. 'We are to work His will.'

So the bright bird of paradise shone in the bleak house and on Sundays in Turner Street. Arias went up all day at the kitchen sink. When Margaret got in from school there was dripping-toast and sweet tea and the great happy smile and the big square teeth ('me teeth's like elephant toes') and jokes about knickers and men, and a dreadfully sweet smell of orange peach powder. 'Nip out an' fetch us ten Goldflakes,' she'd say, and Margaret adoringly would run. On the second

Sunday Marsh prayed for Lydia, by name—Lydia our sister in the Lord—and several of the Saints turned round and smiled at her. She had smiled too and given a sort of royal wave to things temporal and to come, leaning back easily, flexing her feet. Some of the Saints had spontaneously cried out about it, there and then, reminding God that here was matter He ought quickly to be getting to grips with.

And the Saints were quite right, for two Wednesdays later came the first waft of trouble, for as Marsh walked in through his front door at the end of the day his wife hurtled at him from the staircase, her hair on end and her camisole apparent. 'They're not back yet. Kenneth, they're not. They're not back yet.'

'Who?'

'Margaret and Lydia.'

'Where did they go?'

'Well—for the treat.'

'I . . . ' Stick, grey trilby carefully placed in slot and on hook of hallstand, face examined for signs of disorder in hallstand mirror, gloves slapped twice for dust and placed neatly on hallstand shelf—'I am not sure what that is?'

'Oh, Kenneth—it's Wednesday. Lydia takes Margaret for an outing. For a treat . . . '

'Treats. Treats. There is Turner Street.'

'Oh, Kenneth! Turner Street—she's a child.'

'Who is not! "I went with them to the house of God . . . "'

'Kenneth!'

'"—with the voice of joy and praise, with a multitude that kept holiday".'

'But you agreed. You agreed. You remember. Each Wednesday. They've been gone since before two. It's long past six.'

'Well, where did they go?'

'To Eastkirk. I think they always go to Eastkirk.'

'Why Eastkirk?'

'Well, the—seaside.'

'The same sea stands at this front door. Across the promenade.'

'Yes, but a train ride . . . '

'They spend good money.'

'Perfectly straightforward money,' she said flushing. 'Like any other. A shilling or so.'

'A *shilling* or so!'

'But, Kenneth, listen. They're not here. They're not back. They know to be back by five to start the tea.'

'It is precisely ten past six and you are in this state!'

'But there aren't many trains. And Kenneth—I'm afraid. I'm afraid about Lydia. Who is she? Who is she anyway? We should never have kept her. She was sent by mistake.'

'She was sent,' said Marsh. 'She is in God's path.'

'It's Margaret I'm thinking of.'

'Margaret is in God's path already.'

'It doesn't matter whose path she's in if Lydia's a kidnapper.'

'Think what you say please.' His moustache had never looked more tidy, his little neck more tense. There was a gleam about him. She thought, 'He's happy. He likes it. He's got a chance to show how God's in his pocket.' Even while she thought it he put a hand in his pocket and brought out a perfectly square and shiny white handkerchief and shook it out and placed his nose in the centre of the middle crease. He blew into it then whisked the handkerchief about his nostrils. 'The goodness of God endureth continually,' he said, reporting.

'I think what I say,' she said, 'I do think what I say. I think about Margaret and you think about her—Lydia.'

'Naturally I think about Lydia. I believe that Lydia will be saved.'

'You never think about Margaret.'

'This is rubbish.'

'You never have thought about Margaret. Or about me. Or the baby. You just pray and pray for Lydia. The rest of us . . . How do you know what Lydia is?'

'I have been shown,' he said. 'I have been told what to do for Lydia. I am not in my own hands.'

In the dark, narrow, lino-smelling hall the two stood. They glared and Elinor Marsh thought, 'This has not happened before,' and Marsh noted only that a spirit of destructive anxiety had entered his wife and he must pray that she should be restored. 'We'll go in to the sitting room,' he said, 'and be quiet for a moment.'

'I'm frightened for Margaret. Lydia's a whore. You can see she's a whore. She's from nowhere. We are mad. Mad to let Margaret . . . '

'It has been told me,' said Marsh, 'that Lydia has been sent and she is not from nowhere. She is from Bishop Auckland.'

'And it's been told me,' cried his wife in a loud and surprising, rolling rather terrible voice, 'that she is a bad and dreadful and destructive woman.'

She rushed ahead of him into the sitting room with her hand to her face and butted her head into the corner of an over-stuffed sofa. Marsh following saw Margaret and Lydia through the window coming trailing exhaustedly up to the front door. Margaret had her head down and appeared to be playing rather dismally the game where you avoid the lines on the pavement.

'You think,' he said, 'that God had allowed Margaret to be harmed in some way—spirited off—by Lydia?'

'I don't know what I think. I know I'm sounding mad. It's probably after the baby. It's just that I'm frightened of Lydia. I think she might . . . '

'Not bring Margaret back?' He watched Lydia and Margaret through the window. Lydia looked back at him steadily.

'Not just that. I think she might change us. I think she is even changing me already. And I'm wondering what she's teaching Margaret. I'm frightened, Kenneth.'

The front door opened and Lydia's laugh could be heard. With a wobbling silly cry Mrs Marsh ran towards it. 'Oh, they're back! They're here!'

'Stop!' He caught her wrist.

'—or we won't be able to go again,' Lydia was saying in a familiar and validifying voice. 'Well, who cares? Hell, we're late for the bleeding tea.'

'You hear her! You *hear* her,' Elinor said, huge-eyed. 'So now what do you—?'

'I hear her,' he said, 'I hear the work that is in front of me. But I hear nothing that suggests God's abandoning of Margaret. She's safe home.'

'She's home. Whether she's safe . . . '

She fled, past the two girls in the passage, upstairs to the baby taking it up and rocking it though it was already peacefully settled for the night. Margaret watching her run by thought, 'She's silly,' and at the same time, 'It's new. She didn't notice me.' Her mother had given no sign of their mutual love, the secret moppings and mowings, the sign language of the bond between them which Mrs Marsh was so determined that the arrival of the baby should not weaken.

A weight lifted from Margaret's heart. Here might be the beginning of the end of an exhausting contract. Maybe life could soon be ordinary again.

Her father, who never greeted anyone, said, 'Hullo, Margaret. How was Eastkirk? I suppose you missed the train?' Certainly he was not looking at her as he said it so much as at the buttons straining across Lydia's satin blouse. The blouse seemed tighter than ever today. It was thinning under the arms. 'Good afternoon, Lydia.'

'We missed the damn train,' she said. 'I'll get you yer teas afore I tek me things off, so don't fret.' She had to pass very close to Marsh to get to the kitchen. The hard blue buttons touched his chest. He turned and went quickly out of the house, passing Margaret as if she had vanished and Margaret heard Lydia laughing, just out of sight in the kitchen down the dark passage, and the water drumming into the kettle.

Margaret sat down on the hall chair and soon Lydia began to pass to and fro carrying things—ham, a madeira cake and a plate of tomatoes, handfuls of plates and cups—she was casual about trays. At about the seventh trip she gave a scream and dripped milk on her shoes, seeing Margaret watching her in the shadows.

'Help—you scared the living . . . '

Margaret rested her chin in the arc of the walking stick and picked up her father's gloves.

'What yer thinking? Come on—let's hear it then.'

'Nothing.'

'Didn't yer like it? Going off all alone like that. Yer Ma and Pa'd never of let yer go off alone like that. Exploring and that. Had the time o' yer life.'

'You wouldn't have liked it either. If you'd thought.'

'What yer mean, thought?'

'You'd stopped thinking. About me. About anyone. You didn't care where I'd gone as soon as you saw that horrible man.'

'Horrible man—what horrible man? He weren't 'orrible. What man?'

'He was horrible.'

'Just cos I amuse meself—I don't have to give you every minute, do I?'

'No.'

'Well then.'

'But couldn't you see he was horrible?'

'He wasn't 'orrible. He was t'gardener. Up at the 'ouse. The mansion. The *Hall*!'

'Rolling about,' said Margaret into the walking stick.

'What?'

'Rolling.' Her face now in the gloves and turned away.

'You shurrup talking like that.'

'You were,' said Margaret. 'I saw you. When I came down the bank. Him on top. Legs all—white.'

'Shurrup.'

'Yes they were—a lot of white legs. All beastly. Yours—big white hams. *Dents* in. There,' she screamed.

Lydia ran at Margaret dropping the milk jug and smashing it. 'Puckered. Puckered big legs,' yelled Margaret. Milk fountained all over the trilby on the hook down the wall and on to Margaret's smocked dress, excellent at the back. 'All clamped together, rolling, rolling, *rolling*,' shrieked Margaret. 'I hate you, filthy Lydia.' Lydia seized and shook Margaret and began to cry, and up above where Mrs Marsh still dabbed her welling eyes the baby awoke and howled too, and Marsh returning from his steadying brief examination of the sea across the road opened the front door on Lydia with her hands on his daughter's throat, his wife wailing on the stairs and patting abstractedly at the roaring baby. Standing very still he looked at them all and saw milk on his hat.

He thought, 'How primitive. How primitive and strong,' and closed his eyes in prayer to the God of Battles.

# 5.

Upright on the black and red birds sat Marsh with Lydia alongside and Margaret opposite. The day was as hot—it was the following Wednesday—the train as lumbrous and slow, the sun as brilliant, dimming the pictures on the carriage walls and showing up the whiteness of the dust in the curves of the patterned seats, dust which flew puffily about if you beat at the area around it with the flat of the hand. Margaret had been doing this now and then, and at last rather often, and dust blew up into the bars of sunlight and vibrated there. Lydia and Marsh watched. Slap went Margaret. Everyone watched the dust. Slap went Margaret, harder.

'That will do, Margaret. Look at your hand. It will be filthy. "Clean hand and pure heart." Yes?'

Margaret looked at her hand.

'Yes?'

'Psalms.'

'Yes?'

Lydia yawned largely.

'Twenty-four four,' said Margaret.

'Good girl.'

Lydia drew away into her corner. There was a heaviness in the air. Nobody, to look at the three of them, would have guessed they were observing a treat. 'More like a bloody funeral outing, tekkin' flowers to graves an' that,' said Lydia to the Eastkirk geraniums as they got out.

'What was that?' He had been ahead with the tickets.

'Nowt.'

They walked to the promenade and Marsh looked about him. 'And what do you usually do now?' Lydia wandered away and Margaret went and looked out over the wooden bar that fenced the cliff. Behind them young men were riding bikes in smaller and smaller circles. They wore black suits and long white silk scarves and very shiny short hair. Their half-day. They made a lot of noise in the direction of Lydia as usual. Marsh led her away and Margaret followed. 'Can we have ices?' she called.

After thinking about it Marsh bought two very small ice cream cornets and presented them with ceremony. Lydia and Margaret licked unsmiling. In what might have been an attempt to put things right—though in no way interested in why they were wrong—Marsh turned and bought a third ice for himself, but they had run out of cornets and he had to make do with a sandwich. Margaret and Lydia watched his pink tongue sweeping the edges of the wafer to catch the ice cream as it began to ooze in the heat. He managed excellently, his gloves tucked under his arm, but the boys on bikes began to make noises like whooping cough. One quite helpless with laughter fell off.

Shepherding them away from the ungainly sight Marsh asked. 'Where can we go where it is quiet? Shall we walk in the woods?'

'No, the beach. Could we?' Margaret asked fast.

'It looks rather crowded.'

'Could we go on the pier?'

'Wouldn't the woods be cooler? It would be better to sit out of the crowds in the cool.' He looked at Lydia with a quick and meaning eye and she at once set off towards a little hut where you could buy a ticket for a penny ride down to the lower promenade in a box like a greenhouse on a metal rope. The cable-car-greenhouse was at the top, ready and waiting, and Lydia stepped into it. 'Hurry now,' called the man at the wheel and Marsh and Margaret had to follow her. In a stiff row the three descended to the sands of the lower promenade and stepped out into the jostle of the crowds around the entrance to the pier. A penny for the pier it said under a flutter of flags, and sixpence for the pierrots. The pierrots danced and sang for sixpence every hour. 'Oh, could I? Could I?' Margaret clung to Marsh's arm.

'What, the pier? The *pierrots*?'

'Could I see the pierrots?'

She knew at once she had been mad.

'*Dancing*?' he said.

'Yes' (hopelessly). The Saints were not even allowed a wireless set. Spectacles of all kinds were suspect, even God's own. Mind the Book and not the sunset.

'"It is the noise of them that sing do I hear," said Moses, "he saw the calf and the dancing and Moses' anger waxed hot." Where?'

'Exodus,' said Margaret. Once very long ago walking with her mother on the sands she'd seen them—the pierrots—a line of painted people, black and white frills and flounces, rose-red lips, twelve legs and shiny pointed feet all kicking in a line and something had happened like—

'Exodus where?'

'Exodus—' like her mother picking her up and hugging her and swinging her and laughing and her own arms stretching to the wonderful happy noise.

'Exodus *where*?'

When she'd been still quite a baby. 'Exodus thirty-two somewhere. I hate Moses.'

'What!'

'I hate Moses. What about David?'

'How dare you, Margaret!'

'Psalms 150 verses three to six. And what about two Samuel six fourteen?'

'That will do.'

'David danced before the Lord with all his might.'

Lydia scratched her head and then put her hand across her mouth which was grinning and Margaret waited for the end.

'You may go to the pierrots,' said Marsh. Even Lydia gasped.

He took a penny and a sixpence from his pocket and said, 'You may go to the pierrots. You cannot tell Vanity if you have never seen it. The penny is for the turnstile and the sixpence for the performance.'

''Ere,' said Lydia, 'you mean she's to go by 'erself. And me not. She's only *eight*.'

'She will be quite safe.'

'What in all them lot? Chris' they're day trippers 'alf of them from Easington and Shields.'

'They are God's children. They won't harm her. She is in God's path.'

'I'd not bank on that.'

'That,' he said, 'is where you must be set right and whilst Margaret is on the pier you and I will go somewhere quiet and talk about it. Perhaps in the woods?'

'I'm not going in no woods.'

'Mrs Marsh says that you often take Margaret into the woods.'

'I'm not going in no woods with you. I'll leave me place rather than go in any woods with you.'

People were beginning to take an interest. Marsh, fingers between neck and collar said, 'Very well.' He looked about. 'Very well, we will just walk about. Beside the pier. Margaret will be almost within sight on the pier and we shall be walking below.' He took Lydia's plump arm just above the elbow and began to guide her down the steps on to the sands. Margaret saw Lydia looking still very uneasy, truculent even, often looking back. Her big face was angry, as if it were all Margaret's fault. 'Serves her right,' Margaret said and went on to the pier, putting down the penny at the turnstile and all by herself walking through. 'She's got what she deserves so there,' she said as she played the game where you don't step on the lines which is exceptionally difficult on a pier.

And Marsh and Lydia picked their way through the buckets and spades and litter and bodies. When they reached the edge of the sea he let go her arm and they stood looking at the long spars of rock sticking out at an angle from the beach, bright green with seaweed near at hand, black and shiny with wet further out, backed by sudden plumes of spray where the waves hit them further out still. It was a dangerous coast as flat and shallow-looking as a rice paddy but seldom without a wreck sticking up in it somewhere. Even today, as hot as the rest of this burning summer, it was cool by the sea, with few swimmers. Lydia watched the waves spout up beyond the tilted long rocks and rubbed her arm where Marsh had held it. They made an odd couple—one dapper, one gross, and each dressed as if to prove something. They were too heavy for the landscape. Collage on aquatint.

Marsh coughed and said, 'Lydia, let me ask you something.'

She sniffed and humped away, paddling a foot in a pool in the rocks. 'Let me ask you,' he said as she teetered further out, raising his voice a little, 'Have you observed the baby?'

'*Hobserved* the baby?'

'Yes.'

'I don't know what yer talking about.'

'Have you taken notice of the baby?'

'Well acourse I 'ave.'

'You have observed how it cries?'

'I've 'eard it, if that's what you mean. What you talking about? O' course it cries.'

'Ah,' he put up a finger, 'quite so. Exactly. Of course it cries. It is natural for it to cry.'

'Well that's all right then, in' it?' She walked carefully out on the rocks, sat down on one and took off her shoes.

'It is all right that we understand each other,' said Marsh. 'But not exactly all right in any other sense.'

'I don't know what the 'ell you talk about,' she stretched out a leg and began to scrabble up her thigh for suspenders.

'STOP!' Marsh's Sunday voice boomed. 'Lydia, I am talking to you. This is a very serious matter . . . '

'Well, I can listen while I tek me stockin's off. If you think there's somethin' wrong with t'baby yer daft. It's grand. Me Mam's had eight. I should know. I was t'first.'

'Lydia—please. Leave your legs alone—I am talking of original sin.'

'Eh?'

'The baby crying.'

'Horiginal what?'

'Sin. Sin. I am trying to tell you about sin. You know what sin is, Lydia?'

She held a stocking up in the air and regarded it. It had a big sag at the open end. The toe drooped. The rest of it still seemed to hold a leg. Lydia did not often do much about her personal laundry. The queer brown leg hung above the sea and Lydia said, 'In' it a grand shape?'

'Sin,' said Marsh coming closer. 'Have you ever thought about sin, Lydia?'

Still watching the stocking she said, 'Yer cracked.'

'Lydia, Lydia—whenever you have thought about sin I expect you have had a picture in your mind of—lust.'

'Lust?'

'Well—young men on sandhills. The back rows of the cinema. Scarlet women. Now I want you to realise that there is more to it than this. You have heard me preach on Sundays.

Have you, I wonder, begun to understand just what I have been trying to say?'

Lydia took off the other stocking and splashed her toes in a pool.

'Sin,' said Marsh, 'invades every corner of our being. We are born in sin. When you hear the baby cry you hear the cry of sin. Anger, concupiscence, frustration. I will explain. When Margaret was a little girl we had a lawn-mower. If you undid the screws on the lawn-mower the blades came off. Margaret had learned how to unscrew the lawn-mower and she used to trot across the grass and give the screws to her mother as if she had done something clever. We used to say, "No, don't touch the screws, Margaret, and put them back." Then she began to undo the screws and put them in the flower bed. We used to go to the flower bed and bring them back and show her how carefully they needed to be screwed back on. One day she took off the screws and put them in her pocket. "Margaret," we said gently—she was about three years old—"Naughty Margaret. Put back the screws." But she laughed and laughed and ran down the back garden behind the greenhouse and when we fetched her back she was laughing as hard as could be. I carried her back to the lawn-mower—I remember she patted my face all the way. Laughing. Now what do you think I did?'

'Ran her over with the bloody lawn-mower bein' you,' said Lydia.

Marsh closed his eyes for a moment and then picked his way over the seaweedy rocks and stood close to her. He watched her big yellowish feet splashing. He slithered a bit in his shoes.

'What we did was this. Mrs Marsh and I took Margaret aside and explained to her very quietly and slowly, in baby language, exactly why she must never take out the screws again. We reasoned with her. We asked her to give us back the screws. We smiled at her. After a while she took them out of her pocket and gave them to us and watched us put them back on the lawn-mower. And then we kissed her. And I mowed the grass. And what do you think she did next?'

'She fell asleep. Dead bored.'

'No, Lydia. The very next day we saw her go to the lawn-mower when she thought no one was looking, and taking off the screws and with a very serious face she trotted to the dust-bin and THREW THE SCREWS INSIDE! And then she began to put a lot of things on top of them so that we couldn't find them. What do you think this story shows?'

'She didn't like you,' said Lydia.

'No, Lydia, think harder.'

Lydia said nothing.

'She liked long grass p'raps,' said a voice. A boy with a shrimping net was seen to be standing nearby. Lydia began to howl with laughter. 'Come over here,' said Marsh and led the way further out to sea. The boy with the net followed and was soon joined by his sister and then by a stout man with braces and trousers wisely rolled up to the knee. 'The child,' said Marsh trying to disregard his audience and concentrate on his pupil, 'was in the hands of sin.'

'Oh git on,' said Lydia. The girl splashed the boy who held the net and soaked him and he lammed her with it. She began to cry. 'You see,' said Marsh, pointing to the children.

'See what?' said the fat man.

'The force of sin.'

'Shut yer face,' said the man. 'You don't talk to my kids like that. Talk to yer missus how yer like, but you don't bother my kids . . . '

'I was not talking to . . . '

'You was.'

'My friend . . . '

'You're no friend of mine, mate. What you think you are anyway, Jesus Christ or somethin'?'

'I am your friend,' said Marsh with hostility, 'I am talking about sin.'

'Funny place to do it,' said the man. 'In the middle of the sea. In yer best shoes an all. Come 'ere,' he grabbed his children. 'What you want talking to 'im. He's rockers. Git back to yer mother. The tide's comin'in.'

Marsh said, 'My friend, I only wanted to show you—' and stepping forwards off the rock slipped, and fell face down in the water. Lydia's laughter could be heard right over on the beach although it had now become unaccountably much further away. When, still laughing, she had helped him up they seemed further off still and the man and his children were gone back and mingled with the crowds on the shore. 'We'd better look sharp,' she said. 'We'll finish up drowned.' Marsh, sopped all down his front, didn't disagree and let her lead him back through water now nearly up to their knees until they were safe in the shallows. 'Eeeh dear,' she said. 'We're 'avin' a right day. We'll have to get you home somehow, too. Look. Go into a gents, somewhere.' He stood blank.

'You go off into a gents,' she said again, 'and I'll go after Margaret.'

'Sin!' she added. 'Screws!'

He walked thoughtfully out of the water and the boy came up again and watched him. He did not laugh. Several other people were laughing round about but soon they stopped. There was a rather sweet seriousness and unself-consciousness in the small dripping man, and at length a voice, not unkind, shouted, 'You'll have done yer watch in, colonel.' Marsh unhooked the gold watch and chain from his front and examined them. 'Serves him right,' said a less kind voice further off. 'Takin' his girlfriend out there in the current. Undressing on the rocks.' Marsh flushed and Lydia laughed again.

'I don't think she *was* naughty,' said the boy.

'What?' Marsh's alertness sprang back. Up shot his brows.

'The one you were saying about. I don't think that girl was naughty. Hiding them screws. I think she'd just be playing something.'

'You come away from 'im,' yelled the father, coming up.

'He don't know much about playing, son,' said Lydia. To the people on the beach she added, 'Poor sod.'

'Why shouldn't she play with things? Hide and Seek?' said the boy.

'My child,' said Marsh and was off.

He talked.

The boy—a heavy child with a ruminating face—interrupted. Then a woman began. Soon Marsh was surrounded by a little group and when Lydia who had gone off to find Margaret reached the steps up from the beach people were looking back to the group and quite a few were getting up and going over to increase it. Someone asked her if it was an accident. 'That's right,' she said. 'Though he'd not say so.'

'Some soap-box bloke,' said someone else. 'One of these Bible-blokes.'

'No, it's not. It's the Black Shirts.'

'It's the Kensitts.'

'It's only the old Sally Army.'

'It's Punch and Judy.'

'It's yer father,' said Lydia to Margaret who at last emerged dazedly from the pierrots. 'He's found hisself a new Turner Street. E's set for t'rest oft afternoon. What say we go off, you an' me, down the woods?'

## 6.

They hurried through the woods to the bridge and the tree, passing the bandstand in the hollow with barely a glance, down the rough bank to the dry bed of the stream. Lydia had had to put her shoes back on for the walk along the promenade and was grateful to reach the tree to flop down and take them off again. Margaret sat beside her. They were both out of breath as if they had completed an urgent journey. As they recovered, Margaret first, they looked about them into the trees.

'Off yer go then,' said Lydia.

'Where?'

'Wherever it is yer go.'

'Don't you mind?'

'No—yer safe 'ere. Not like with yon riff-raff ont' pier.'

'No, I mean don't you mind being alone?'

'No. I'm grand.'

'But I've had the pierrots. I'll keep with you if you like. I've had my treat.'

Picking her teeth Lydia looked at Margaret suddenly, took hold of her chin and then patted her face. 'Go on. Have another treat too,' she said. 'Yer bonny.'

'It's not a *treat*,' said Margaret.

'Well it's not lectures about lawn-mowers.'

'What?'

'Nowt. You git off now.'

'Oh—you mean in case he comes?'

'I mean nowt of the sort. We've only got ten minutes. In case who comes?'

'That man—you *know*! You only got your hands round my throat that's all. You know—don't pretend.'

They both wondered quickly at how close they had grown and the things their friendship could bear. 'You go on about that man,' said Lydia not quite meeting Margaret's eyes, 'I'm just here easin' me feet.'

'Father . . . '

'He's right. He's grand. Don't you fret. He's settin' them all straight. An'll not be ten minutes.'

Halfway up the bank Margaret called, 'You'll be lonely if he doesn't come,' but Lydia turned her back and leaned against the tree, twirling her toes. Margaret at the top of the bank could still see the toes moving. She thought, should I have said come too, and then realised no. Most certainly not.

Excitement took over as she came out of the trees—a reminiscent excitement. The light over the vast yellow lawn flooded into view and she remembered. It was like a curtain going up, but quite different from the pierrots.

There was the mansion and there again was the man under the trees seated at his painting. It was later in the afternoon than it had been the other time and there were shadows on the grass and down the side of the great house. She noticed a large, rather ramshackle conservatory to one side of it with arched panes of glass, finials and spikes and white wrought iron and a mass of dark within. As she stood just out of sight at the lawn's edge the door of the conservatory was flung open and a troop of people burst out. They began to walk two by two across the grass. They were both men and women, about twenty of them trooping together raggedly, talking and laughing. Some of them were holding hands and swinging their arms. 'Like school,' she thought.

'Like a baby school! But they're grown-ups. Some of them are even old.'

The troop came marching over the grass towards her for a little way, then veered off in the direction of the artist, who paid them no attention. As they drew nearer to him and to Margaret she could hear them laughing and chattering and saw that they all wore the same sort of clean but faded clothes—lineny, cottony, thin sort of clothes, washed but not ironed, washed away into pale pinks and blues and lavenders and whites. Almost a uniform. But not a costume. The pierrots had had a costume—all shiny and ironed. A lot of these had white puffy hair all clean but not arranged. They stopped and gathered round the artist and the chattering grew louder as they pushed forward, closed in, though he still appeared to take no notice, looking up now and then as usual at the house, dabbing minutely with the long brush. The people in the cluster in their pale clothes looked like hydrangeas, thought Margaret, like our hydrangeas in the back garden where I played hunt the thimble with the lawn-mower screws and they all went mad. She felt that the people were perfectly lovely—happy and good-tempered, needing each other and hand in hand.

Someone in dark clothes appeared from somewhere with outstretched arms and the troop of people trotted away across the grass again. Heads nodded as the procession was shepherded round the flank of the house to another door and out of sight. When they had gone it was as if a breeze had dropped.

She wondered whether to go on round behind the man, like last time. She was beginning to want to get nearer to him and look at the picture. She did not at all want to get nearer to the kitchen garden and turned her mind away from it and the awful thing inside it; but the man seemed to have a comfortable and accepting look as if perhaps he knew that she was there.

Then he slowly bent down and began to pack up his paints, clean up his palette. Very slowly he loosened the picture in the easel, let the easel down and packed it, together with the box and his camp stool. Holding the painting from below on a spread hand he moved off across the grass. He moved lightly for such a stout man, his short fat trousers fining down to points at the feet.

The door of the conservatory shut behind him and the scene was over.

Lydia, whose foot no longer twirled, she found grumpy and ready to go. 'Pull us up,' she said. 'Eeeh, we're that daft. There'll be merry'cll.' Marsh, when they looked for him over the promenade railings, was no longer on the beach, and the beach was gone, too. The tide sloshed at the sea wall. The pier was empty, the ice cream kiosk all barred up. It was clearly very late indeed. There was no sign of Marsh at the station either and they approached Seaview Villas anxiously.

But all was calm. Mrs Marsh was making the tea. She kissed Margaret. 'Somehow or another your father missed you, dear. He came back alone. I hope you didn't worry, Lydia! He's had to go out again. He's so pleased, so *pleased*, dear! He preached on the sands at Eastkirk and gathered quite a crowd. He says he is going to start something there every week. "Hang the Bank", he said.

"Hang the Bank!" He's just gone round to Turner Street to arrange for hymn sheets and the megaphone.'

Margaret ate her baked beans.

'Did you have a lovely time? Was it a lovely treat? Father said be allowed you to see the *pierrots*—wasn't that marvellous? Wasn't it lovely of him? Were they wonderful?'

Margaret thought of the hydrangea people on the yellow lawn. 'I'd nearly forgotten the pierrots,' she said.

'That's right,' said her mother boiling groats for the baby, busy at the stove.

'I suppose it is,' said Margaret.

'What?'

'Nothing. Filthy groats. They do smell. Baby smell.'

'Here,' said Ms Marsh and slid a fried egg on to the baked beans. 'Margaret's favourite. Treat for a good girl.'

Margaret looked at it, shiny, slippery, a frilly sea-weed edge, the frothy curly mark the waves leave behind them, but hot and luscious. She touched it with her fork and it dented in like a breast. 'What are you thinking, sweet Margaret!' Mrs Marsh, riding along on her husband's recent benignity, swept down and enveloped her.

'That everyone's mad!' Margaret shouted. She pushed first her mother, then the egg and beans away and ran from the room. She sat on the hall chair kicking at the hallstand in the gloom. She thought about the mansion and its flood of light and happy people. She wondered two Corinthians five one whether she had seen a house not made with hands, eternal in the heavens.

'I'm not coming after you, Margaret,' came from the kitchen and from pursed and insulted lips.

## 7.

She walked right up to the painter this time, no nonsense. She walked right up over the grass in the blaze of the day, and stood looking at him. His brush tap-tapped at the canvas and he creased his eyes and paid her not the slightest attention and she walked nearer and at last even put out a finger to the edge of the canvas, standing alongside, not looking at it but at his face.

'Drinkwater,' he said at last. He painted on.

'I'm Margaret.'

'Ah.'

'I'm Margaret Marsh, I'm eight.'

'Seen you about. Wondered if you'd be dropping over.'

'Not exactly dropping . . . '

'No. Skulking about in the fronds.'

'Fronds?'

'The edge of the forest.'

Margaret sat down on the grass and began to pull up blades of it. They were short and dusty. She thought about fronds and the forest. They were funny sorts of words.

'Skulking about,' he said, 'and off to the kitchen gardens. Not much joy there.'

'No.'

'*Not* much joy,' he said and laughed. His face was fat with round red pads for cheeks above the beard. The panama hat was old and limp but clean. His eyes were blue and simple and clear like a baby's. '*Not* much joy,' he repeated. 'Tell me, d'you find that?'

'What?'

He stopped painting and looked at her for a long while. 'How d'you do,' he said again. 'Name's Drinkwater.'

'I'm Margaret.'

'Ah.'

He went back to the painting with a detachment so complete that she felt physically dismissed, wiped off the grass like a colour, but there was such peace in his presence that she put up no fight against this and sat on, pulling grass, and eventually lay down on it, rolling about rather, spreading her arms. She looked at the sky, then back over at the edge of the wood. Beyond seemed impossible. Lydia seemed impossible. Home seemed impossible. It didn't exist.

And it was so very hot. 'I am beyond myself,' thought Margaret.

'D'you know . . . ' she began to talk to Mr Drinkwater, 'how they say you get beyond yourself? It's a funny thing to say. Go to bed at once they say, you're beyond yourself. They don't want to know anything about it. D'you know why? It's because they're frightened. They're frightened of you. They don't know how to deal with you. Deal with you. The way they talk to children—they get angry because they're frightened. Of children.'

'They've stopped being frightened here,' said Mr Drinkwater.

'Why do they get so angry though?' Margaret ruminated on.

'Firm,' said Drinkwater. 'It's more firm than angry. Here. They've got their little ways. They've got their special voices.'

'My mother's got a special voice.'

'Ah.'

'It's her teaching voice. It's her voice for improving me. Why can't she just—not?'

'Just not,' said Drinkwater. 'Exactly. *Exactly.*'

He stopped painting and put a hand on each knee, the brush in one hand and the palette in the other. He looked long and excitedly at Margaret widening his bright eyes. He nodded his head and looked at her rolling on the grass as if she were a new country he had just come upon over an unpromising horizon—a country of great wonder and satisfaction. 'My dear young lady,' he said, 'why can't they just not?'

'I've got a brother,' she said, 'a baby. He wasn't born all that long ago. About eight weeks. He's all slobbery and wobbly. His head lolls about. There's a soft bit in the top of it with a pulse beating. All he does is suck and cry and sleep. They're calling him Terence. I don't like that, do you? I think that Terence is an awful name. And they go on and on, how do you like Terence, Margaret? No? Then what name would *you* like him to have? As if they'd change it! And then my mother moons at me with one of those looks. You know.'

'Oh, I know.'

'I'd like Scummy,' she said, 'Scummy, Scummy, Scummy.'

'Don't care much for that.'

'I don't care for the baby.'

'Pooh,' he said. 'Babies. I've seen very few of them lately.'

'You can see in her eyes,' said Margaret, 'she thinks "I'm being very, very kind to Margaret in case she's jealous of the BABY".'

'Kind though,' said Drinkwater. 'You've got to admit that. They're very kind. They do it here. Oh, a great deal of the time. Most of the day. And in the evenings.'

'At night, too,' said Margaret. 'My mother comes to say goodnight. Usually with the baby. Patting it. Its head rolls around. And then my father comes in for prayers.'

'Ah, that might be better.'

'Do you have prayers?'

A look of immense sadness flooded over Mr Drinkwater and seemed to shrink him. He sank down into his linen suit and his stomach jutted forward more than before and his beard lay on his chest. He sat brooding on his feet and Margaret noticed for the first time that he was wearing large wellington boots.

'There are no prayers here,' he said, 'at least not public ones. We have a Chaplain. Welshman. Very Low. No good at all. Trouble of course with these places is that the staff get as bad as the inmates. Have you ever noticed that? Everyone's the same in six months—maids, cooks, bottle washers. Not many bottle washers mind. Don't know when I've seen a feller washing a single bottle. Can't talk to the Chaplain—lives in the lodge with a mouse.'

'With a *mouse*?'

'Called a wife. Holy lot.'

'Oh—is he a Primal Saint?'

'Yes, I'm sure he is.'

'A Primal Saint? *Is* he? We are. At home. But it's very rare, my father says. He says we are God's Elect.'

'A good deal of praying there then, I dare say? A good fat portion of that sort of thing?'

'Yes. Well, there has to be.'

'I suppose so.'

'Being rare.'

'God's Elect.'

'Yes.'

'I wouldn't say the Chaplain was God's elect.'

'Well, p'raps you're wrong then. Perhaps he's not a Primal Saint?'

'He's a fucking fool,' said Mr Drinkwater, and shook himself. Emerging from the depths of his linen jacket he began to paint again very vigorously with enormous swashes, leaning about on the stool, swinging about masterfully.

'Can I look at the picture?' Margaret asked after a pause while she tried to get used to the shock. Drinkwater did not reply. 'If my father had heard you say that,' she said . . .

Drinkwater flung a gout of cobalt blue at the canvas and began to whistle with little puffing noises through fat lips.

'My father,' said Margaret briskly and sitting up, dusting herself, regarding him sternly, 'would say you *need* prayers. That was an awful thing to say.'

'Ah.'

'About the Chaplain. Just awful. It's the sort of thing that Lydia says—p'raps not even Lydia. And she can't help it. She comes from Bishop Auckland. It's very terrible at Bishop Auckland. She can't help it. But you . . . '

'You oughtn't,' she said again and heard her voice accusing. 'I mean, I know I sound like them, saying it . . . '

'Like them?'

'Yes, people. When they send you to bed and say you're beyond yourself.'

'Beautiful phrase, isn't it?'

'Well, that's what I said. That's how we started. We said at the beginning. Don't you remember?'

He looked at her.

'We said. You agreed. They go all kind and firm and say you've got beyond yourself—you must remember. It's what we . . . '

His face became suddenly happy as could be and he nodded in welcome. 'Name's Drinkwater,' he said. 'Who are you?'

'I think you're mad,' she said and stamped round the easel and stood behind him to see what he had made of the house.

The big yellow monster slept in the sun, its red leaves creeping, its fine strong chimney bricks and its deep old roof and grey-green leads and gutter pipes all scrolled with coats of arms—a lovely house across the grass and all very quiet.

She looked at the painting. It was a tangled nest of snakes, fat lipped and over-lapped with scales, glutinous eyes, pink-mouthed, thickly coiled like a boiling of limbs for cannibals. The last strokes of cobalt were daubed anywhere, disfiguring but not hiding the careful brushwork of the reptiles which, as Margaret looked at them, seemed to multiply, denser and denser, into circles diminishing in the distance until they were too far off to be seen.

# 8.

Mr Marsh's success at the first of his prayer meetings on the sands so delighted him that the next week, when Margaret had met Mr Drinkwater, he had been more ambitious. Although Wednesday was a weekday it was early-closing and he was able to muster several Saints who were shopkeepers. One Saint who manned the lifeboat on occasions was also available and of great help in noting the tides to ensure that Marsh and his disciples could establish themselves on a patch of sand which would not disappear during the course of the service. Five ladies of sombre appearance all wearing hats and carrying sheet music mustered here too, with the shopkeepers. A Saint with an interesting large head held the bag. He was fiftyish and appeared rather simple as a result of the Somme, but was of invaluable use wherever he went because of the huge spread of his smile. He looked perfectly normal from a distance and could sing in tune. Had he been mentally damaged before and not after the war he might have put the whole thing to an end in no time. The great waves of his benignity made disagreements cease.

When Marsh had got going on the megaphone and the ladies in hats had struck up the hymn and the simple Saint had began to clink the bag up and down and grin, a very amiable feeling spread about. Sandcastles were left half-moated, newspapers lowered and laid aside and people sucking peppermint rock or mooning about wondering whether to paddle or not began to gather round. Some people even splodged out of the sea landwards, skirts held up above purplish knees, trousers rolled above ropish veins. Several men in caps who stood all day long like war memorials by the fishing boats, with deep lines on their faces and shiny, desperately maintained suits—the unemployed—turned to see what the old geezer was up to, and a pale boy, a butcher's messenger Marsh was said to have been good to, suddenly struck up on the trumpet like the rip of doom.

'Bringing in the sheaves,' announced Marsh. Heads nodded and tambourines jingled and ten voices cried out nearly together:

'Bringing in the sheaves
Bringing in the sheaves
We shall come rejoicing
Bringing in the sheaves.'

A pause. Deep breathing. More nods. A moment's silence through which the pale jingling of the pierrots blew like a ghost. Then WHAM! Two trumpets, three megaphones, ten lungs of the ladies in hats, tambourines, the accurate and surprisingly strong baritone of Marsh and the formidable bass of the simple one declared furiously to the ocean and everything near it that they were bringing in corn for harvest. It was really rather fine. Even the people on the pier clustered to the rail with their backs to the paid entertainment.

The next week it was even better but different. It was not at Eastkirk but on the sands outside Marsh's own door and the group was embellished by the presence of Lydia—Lydia sitting at Marsh's feet on a kitchen chair brought down from the house. Marsh behind her had climbed a little rostrum taken from Turner Street and was smart as paint in his best suit. Lydia in the blue sateen, huge and beautiful, sat with a perplexed and rather sullen look not at all like herself, and beside her the baby's big black pram, leathery as a hansom cab, harsh as an old beetle. On her knee lay the baby itself, spread out sleeping, its purple crescent eye-lids shut and every other bit of it wrapped up in shawls and bonnets and mitts and bootees according to the custom of the time. Lydia held it loosely—yet safely. Her hands knew perfectly that they must not fall away from it, yet her deepest attention was certainly somewhere else. She gazed flatly out into the gathering crowd like a huge over-painted Memlinc madonna.

'Bringing in the sheaves,' cried the Saints with not too bad a beat, and slowly the crowd joined in. The bag began to clink. The Westkirk dole men by the boats turned their heads, ladies surprised themselves with forgotten sopranos, and God was set going like mad against the withdrawing tide.

A success—and because of it Margaret and her mother found themselves this Wednesday alone together. Mrs Marsh could never quite bring herself to appear on the beaches. Also her milk was beginning to dry up and a visit to her doctor had suggested that perhaps some underlying anxiety was the cause. He suggested rest and some relaxation.

'There is of course no need to breast feed any more,' he said. 'You have done nearly three months. The child is very well.'

'I believe in breast feeding. I fed Margaret for ten months.'

'In the jungle they breast feed for two years. I suppose if you wish you could go on for ten. Socially however . . . '

Mrs Marsh did not speak but flushed. There was something indelicate. Also trivial. The Saints did not take account of social matters.

'Mrs Marsh,' he said, 'I suggest some bottles of milk for the baby and some social life for yourself. Go out with your daughter. You must not neg . . . '

'Oh, I am very careful,' she said. 'I am not a fool, doctor. I have been very careful of that. Margaret and I are very close. We have no secrets. She has never been neglected.'

'She needs,' said the doctor who knew about the Primal Saints, 'a little fun, you know.'

'She goes out every Wednesday with our maid—hardly more than a child herself. Not eighteen. They are great friends.'

'Couldn't you take her out? The two of you ought to be free of the baby sometimes. Isn't there some friend . . . ?'

So the Wednesday when the rest of the family established itself on the sands Mrs Marsh and Margaret set out to tea with the Fraylings in Dene Close.

Margaret was in the dress with pretty smocking and Mrs Marsh in an old loose crêpe-de-chine two-piece with a long scarf to match which she had had on her honeymoon twelve years ago and scarcely worn. They locked and left the house with a feeling of uncertainty, not so much at what they were doing but because of the clothes, and Mrs Marsh looked at herself several times in the big ugly windows of Seaview Villas as they went along.

It was so queer to be out without the pram, the one long-legged child holding her hand and not the pram handle. At eight Mrs Marsh realised that hand-holding with Margaret was nearly over. She looked down at Margaret's face. It was unsmiling and thoughtful and she squeezed the hand hard.

'Lovely going out together, just us two.'

Margaret did not reply.

'Too big to hold my hand?' She leaned down, conspiratorially, 'Oh come on now, Margaret. Answer me.'

Margaret said that she was trying not to speak until she had got to the tea place.

'But, darling, why not?'

No answer.

'Darling—have I upset you, angel?'

'Oh, shut up,' Margaret lunged off from her mother's hand. 'I was *playing*.'

'I'm sorry I'm sure,' said Elinor. They crossed over the sandhills and into a formal and rather nasty-looking park with prominent litter-bins and bright green council seats and benches. Dene Close was just beyond.

'Since we're a little early, shall we sit down?' said Mrs Marsh, 'and you can tell me all about what you and Lydia do when you go out with her.'

'No, let's get on.'

'I don't like to be too early.'

'Oh let's,' said Margaret.

'No, dear. She may still be changing.'

'Changing!'

'Yes, dear, Binkie always changes in the afternoons.'

(From what? Into what? Spiders? Fairies? Serpents? Houses could become snakes.)

'At least I'm sure she always used to.'

'Could I go home?' said Margaret.

'Darling, no! Don't you like being with me?'

'Yes, but . . . '

'You don't want to run home when you're out with Lydia.'

'No. I know. But . . . '

'Darling—do you like being with Lydia more than with me?'

In the green crêpe-de-chine, low-waisted and sloping shouldered, with the romantic trailing scarf Mrs Marsh sat down on the ugly seat and looked terribly sadly down at her greenish silk stockings. Tears welled up.

'Oh, for heaven's sake,' said Margaret and flounced off out of the park, with her mother in a moment running after her.

'What is it you do when you're with Lydia that's so nice?' she begged at the kerb.

'Not anything. Oh, do shut up.'

'Everything seems special about Lydia.'

'I don't think about her. I don't bother with her when I'm out at all if you want to know,' said Margaret. They had reached number three Dene Close and stood before a chromium knocker, boot-scraper, letter-box, and door handle and a door which had the rising sun in stained glass panels bursting from the bottom left-hand corner. 'What a door! Ghastly.'

'Ssh! Darling! Yes, I know.' Torn between delight at Margaret's revelation about Lydia and her reaction to the commonness of the door she suddenly enveloped her daughter on the step. 'Oh, my darling,' she laughed, turning very pretty, 'hush.'

'She's quite right,' said a man's voice behind them just as the door opened in front, 'Hello, Elinor. Hello, Miss Marsh.' He was smiling at them both, a tall, easy-looking man, thin, with a soft moustache. His eyes were sweet and gentle. Margaret knew in this first glance at him that whoever he was he liked her mother very much.

'Hello, Charles.'

Her mother had looked quickly at the man and then away.

'Hello, Elinor.' The sun-ray door was open and a big strong-looking woman with square shoulders was on the inside of it, drying her hands on a tea-cloth. She wore a blouse and skirt and very heavy shoes. 'You're early. I haven't changed. But I wasn't going to.'

'Oh, I'm sorry. Of course not.'

'Given it up,' said the woman glaring at Elinor's crêpe-de-chine. 'Don't you agree? Come in. And I've stopped a maid.'

'Goodness,' said Elinor. 'I haven't done that yet.'

'The times are changed instead of Binkie,' said Charles. 'Farewell sweet maids.'

'Well, I hope that Binkie will never change for me,' said Elinor. She caught Margaret staring at her and said quickly,

'Oh—this is Margaret, Binks. I didn't bring the baby. The baby's on the sands.'

'Good,' said the woman. 'I like little girls and I hear the baby's a boy. Come with me.' She thrust out a hand and took Margaret into the kitchen and sat her on a chair before a table on which was a knife, a bowl of butter-filling, and a wire rack with yellow sponge buns on it. 'Cut off the top of each bun,' she said. 'Go on. That's it. Turn it on its side and slice. Now then, paste a thick blob of filling on the new top, wipe the knife, and cut the little circle you've cut off in half. Now, dab it like a butterfly into the filling. It is a butterfly cake.'

Margaret smiled.

'Clever girl. Pretty fingers. Now, do fourteen more while I make tea and uncover the sandwiches. How many buns is that altogether?'

'Fifteen.'

'And how many people?'

'Well, two.'

'No—for tea.'

'Oh—four.'

'So how many each?'

'Oh—not quite—oh—four I suppose.'

'Wrong!' said the square woman happily. 'You're relying on all kinds of most unlikely things. For instance everybody being equally hungry.'

'It was tables,' said Margaret.

'Tables are all very well,' said the woman, 'but they take no account of whims.' She swung about the kitchen on her stout legs and Margaret watched her and wondered why such a bossy woman didn't annoy her. The kitchen was very clean and sunny and all the tins were painted different colours. There were bright checked curtains and a lot of plants on the window-sill above the sink. The whole kitchen was yellow with sun. There was a smooth and comforting Aga cooker, a row of cake-tins with flowers on, labelled sponge, fruit, madeira; shallower tins for biscuits, and whenever the woman opened and shut cupboards, rows of very clear glass bottles and jars with coloured things in them, and all labelled, were seen to be standing at the ready in very straight rows. There were several tea-caddies and the woman opened them all and took a spoonful from each and put them one by one into a silver tea pot with an acorn on its lid for a knob. The quickness and sureness and kindness of the woman made Margaret begin to slice up the buns and turn them into butterfly cakes without any self-consciousness at all and she heard herself say in her Lydia or Drinkwater voice, 'In the afternoons—what was it you usually changed into?'

'Oh—any old thing. It was just a habit. By the way I'm called Binkie. My brother's Charles.'

'I expect mother would . . . '

'What?'

'Oh—well. I expect I ought to call you Mrs something. Frayling.'

'I don't,' said the woman, 'Mrs Frayling is my mother. And Charles's. I'm a miss, thanks be.'

'Don't you want to get married?'

'Too old now.'

'Your brother isn't . . . ' Margaret thought about it, 'married either?'

'No.'

'I wouldn't think he was too old.'

'No.'

'It's a bit unusual though.'

'It is rather.'

'He's so . . . '

'What?'

'So lovely,' said Margaret.

Binkie gave her a swift glance as she poured boiling water

on the tea. 'I'm glad I've met you,' she said. 'You're a nice little girl. Come along. Help me pull the trolley in. Put the butterflies on the bottom shelf. Be careful.'

She raised her voice rather as they crossed the hall and made a clumsy sort of noise opening the door. 'A useful girl,' she called out to her brother and Elinor, who were sitting very far apart and silently in the long sitting-room. 'She is a record breaker at butterfly-cakes.' Charles had stood up when they came into the room and did not sit down until Margaret had sat down on the chesterfield beside her mother. 'Can one break cakes?' he said thoughtfully.

'Yes,' said Elinor thoughtfully back.

'Doesn't breaking imply noise?' he asked with the same frowning crossword-puzzle air.

'Not necessarily,' she said.

'What breaks silently?'

'Well, bread. Breaking of bread.'

'There is a tearing noise. Anyway—archaic?'

'Dawn,' she said.

'Different meaning. A metaphor.'

'Snow,' she said. 'Avalanches—bits of snow breaking off. Quite silent.'

Margaret looked from face to face like a person at a tennis match. She knew—though heaven knew how—that this game had been played before and very often and very happily. The tennis match idea stayed with her and she had a queer picture of her mother and Mr Frayling playing tennis with careful slow strokes on a summer evening with the shadow of the net growing long across the grass. Some people stood watching from a distance. Perhaps some old photograph.

'Do you and Mummy play this?' Charles Frayling asked her with his head on one side, as if to catch her answer exactly. Still muddled with tennis, she looked at her mother.

'I don't think we do, do we, dear?' Elinor said.

'Not ever.'

'Try,' said Charles. 'It's called the grand great word game.'

'The great *grand* word game,' said Elinor.

'Yes. Sorry. Great grand. Try, Margaret. What breaks without a noise?' He looked out of the window and said as if he was not listening for a reply, 'It's been rather long. I'm out of practice. What breaks silently?'

'Hearts,' said Margaret.

There was a quick, electric pause.

'Rubbish,' said Binkie, 'I don't believe in broken hearts.' Elinor, who had turned rosy, crumbled her butterfly-cake and said neither did she.

'But it is not rubbish,' said Charles and Margaret noticed that he was the only one who had seen her discomfort and bewilderment and that they were growing worse the less she understood them. Tears had even come into her eyes. 'Hearts do break silently,' said Charles.

'No. A different meaning again,' said Elinor, cheeks cooling down. 'Like dawn, you wouldn't let me have dawn and I won't let you have hearts. Metaphor was never allowed.'

'Metaphor,' said Charles to Margaret, 'means a way of saying something by using a picture. It's called an image. You make a picture of a heart breaking in two, you see, to say that someone is unhappy. It can't of course happen in fact.'

'It can,' said Margaret, suddenly angry at the man's patient schoolmasterish kindness. 'Father said it happened to Jesus on the Cross. That's the meaning of water and blood John nineteen thirty-four. When the centurion put the sword in there issued forth water and blood. That is because Jesus died of a broken heart. It's a thing surgeons know and it's what they call it when they aren't using the long doctor's name for it. It's a broken heart and compare Luke six forty-five.'

There was now a very long silence in the room.

'And anyway,' said Margaret. 'Father doesn't like her to be called Mummy.'

Walking back through the park and along the sea front she was jaunty and defiant. She walked ahead and clattered a stick she had picked up against the litter-bins, one by one. On the Front she ran about the sand dunes and then along the stone wall that flanked the sands. She determinedly did not look at her mother, and appeared oblivious and arrogant about the slight droop of the crêpe-de-chine trailing along behind her.

It occurred to her now and then in flashes that something had gone badly wrong with the afternoon, but by the time she had reached the end of the stretch of dunes she found that she believed that her rudeness at the end of the visit, though horrific to people who had offered friendliness and puzzles and butterfly-cakes, was the least part of it. Things had happened which she knew quite certainly were not her fault. They related to other things that had happened a long time ago, and secrets. She knew that the tea-party had been an attempt at a bridge back to some of these old events, had been an event in itself of great delicacy and fearfulness to—whom?

To her mother rather than to the man, she thought. He seemed so wise and strong, though saddish. To her mother then—for the sister Binkie was certainly not fearful at all. You felt that she had had her say a good time ago and was proceeding sensibly. Her feet were on the earth and her life yielding fruit Genesis one eleven. No, it was her mother who had had to endure most during the afternoon as a result of something that had happened a great time ago. And she had taken Margaret along as a safeguard. A foil. And Margaret had disgraced her.

'I am a disgrace,' she thought.

She stopped half-way along a slatted seat which faced the sea. It had a metal ticket nailed to its back saying that it had been given in memory of someone dead in the war to enable others to rest. 'Get down off that seat,' a man shouted. 'Walking all over it with your filthy feet.' Margaret in her smocked dress and polished shoes hung her neat head. She deserved this. She had been a disgrace. She accepted everything. She got down. 'Children,' said the man angrily to her mother who had come up with them.

Elinor took Margaret's hand and said that she had only been playing.

'Play. That's it. That's the trouble.' He shambled off.

'Dreadful creature!' She kept tight hold of Margaret. 'Dreadful. He's that gassed man—that crank. Whatever's his name?'

'It's Bezeer-Iremonger. He's one of Father's.'

'Good gracious. He is. How angry he looked. He's so gentle usually. He must be getting worse. What can have upset him? He seems to get all over the place these days. Or maybe it's just that all of them get the same in the end—the ones that got back from the war. Wander about. I believe he was in a sort of Home for a long time, poor soul. He is always so docile—how very odd.'

'Mother . . . '

They walked along.

'Mother—I'm sorry.'

'It's all right,' she said.

'I just felt . . . '

'Never mind, darling. I know. He's so . . . '

'He was so—sort of understanding. That man Charles.'

'He was. Always.'

'Always? I've never seen him before.'

'He was my—best friend. When I was little.'

'How little?'

'Oh—five I suppose.'

'Until when?'

'Until—well, until I married your father.'

'Father's a bit different.'

'Yes.'

'Actually—*you* are very understanding.'

'I'm glad, darling.'

'No—I mean, like him. I wish you weren't sometimes. It makes me feel—just that I'll never be good enough.'

'You father should be able to deal with that.' Elinor's voice was sharp. It hurt. It was not comfortable.

In the distance they both watched a little dump of people coming up off the beach, in the middle of it the flash of a trumpet and the white flap of sheet music. A baby's pram detached itself from them and then Lydia—her hair a golden blob even at that distance.

The pram and the blob drew away from the others and then a single figure walking urgently followed them. Marsh's short-legged, hustling steps which could never quite free themselves into strides reached Lydia quickly, and appeared to complete a family trio which crossed the road towards Seaview Villas.

'There's Daddy.'

'Father.'

'Yes. I didn't like him saying "Mummy".'

'Charles? Are we talking about Charles now?'

'Yes.'

'Well you made that clear, dear.'

'I've said I'm . . . '

'You could write a little note.'

'I'd write to her—the sister.'

'You were not rude to her.'

'But I wasn't rude to him. Only telling him about Jesus's heart. Daddy—Father would of . . . '

'Would have.'

'Wouldn't he?'

'He—but he would never, never, never have gone there to tea.' She sighed.

'Why?'

'Well—they don't believe in . . . As a matter of fact you see they, the Fraylings, actually hate the—Saints.'

'Well, so does Lydia.'

'They argue outright about it though. You see, they're very clever, the Fraylings.'

'But isn't Daddy?'

'Father. He is not clever like Charles and Binkie, dear. He's not educated like them. He has always lived here, you see. He's never lived anywhere else.'

'Do you have to leave a place to be clever?'

Mrs Marsh thought about it. They too were up to the end of Seaview Villas now, and walked more slowly as they neared home. 'I believe you do in a way,' she said. 'It's because I never went away that no one here will ever think I'm clever. Charles and Binkie were at Cambridge.'

'What's Cambridge?'

'A place for clever people.'

More that anything that had happened during the afternoon—more than anything that had happened since the baby came, perhaps in her whole life, this astonished Margaret. Her parents, it appeared, were not clever. They had never been away and they were not clever.

'I think, you see . . . ' Mrs Marsh put on the abominably kind face, the slow understanding voice of the man. 'I think . . . '

'Oh it's all right,' Margaret yelled. 'I'm going to catch up Lydia. Bye,' and she rushed off down the road. Her mother joined her on the doorstep—for it was much too late to catch Lydia, of course, and she had no key. Mrs Marsh said, 'I think, you see, that everyone should get a bit beyond . . . '

Lydia was lifting the baby from its folds. The black pram

suited the hall. Marsh stood in the gloom, alert in his dark suit, and spoke sombrely.

'They sang from the heart.'

Lydia turned away.

'I hope you had a nice tea-party, Elinor?'

Margaret thought, No, he's not very clever. He is not. But, poor thing, he tries to be good. Then she was filled with guilt at such a cool and unloving thought.

'I was weighing him up,' she thought, 'as if he was just anyone.' She went to him and put both arms round his waist. He took no notice but went on talking above her head, only putting his hand on her hair a moment before pushing her away.

'There isn't a thing I could tell him,' she thought. 'Not a thing he would listen to. He's as bad as that man Charles who listened too much.'

She thought of Mr Drinkwater who had listened and considered to perfection, had understood utterly, though patchily because his memory had kept slipping. He had given her deep attention even while so busy with the snakes, and being so upset. The snakes showed just how upset he had been. He had not been wanting to spoil the house with snakes—he had just been showing how awful things could be—how the house could be strangled up by snakes. He knew that poisonous things could stand side by side with heaven. The creature in the wicker box, in all her horror, had lain looking at the apple tree and the deep blue sky.

Still talking, her father pushed her away. In the hall was the smell of warm baby and some rabbit stock boiling much too hard on the kitchen stove. The huddle of big people above her head cluttered the narrow space. She thought of Drinkwater's bright face, the marvellous space he had sat in, the burnt gold grass, the great dry lake of lawn, the queer procession, the fierce dark nurse, the huge brilliant living eyes of the flat woman in the basket.

'I have been away,' she thought. 'She doesn't know—none of them know. I've been away already. I'm cleverer already.'

'That lass is clemmed,' said Lydia. 'Fair clemmed to death. Tired out. Look at her. Thin and done. Neither back nor belly. Look at her!'

'I'm all right.'

'She does look tired,' said Elinor, surprised.

''Ere,' said Lydia and dumped Terence into his mother's arms. 'Jus' you see to 'is bottle, missis. I's puttin' that Margaret into her bed.'

# 9.

It was more than a week before Margaret left the house again, for when she woke up the morning after the outing to Dene Close it was to know that something was badly wrong. Her neck hurt and her head was not eager to move about on it. It did not feel ready to raise itself from the pillow without the neck's aid. It lay there like a head of lead or stone, like the head of a prone monument. Carefully she felt the neck. There was a great deal more of it than yesterday. The head ached and the light coming through the thin curtains was too bright. Lydia came in and drew them back, making it torture, and said that she must get up quick. Breakfast was ready. Whatever was the matter—Margaret who was always down first?

'Ow,' said Margaret shielding her eyes, and Lydia yelled, 'Lord above, what's this?'

Mrs Marsh arrived with the baby curled on her dressing-gowned shoulder, gave a gasp and cried, 'I'll come back. I must put him down.'

'Mumps, darling,' she whispered then from the bed's foot. 'Mumps,' she said turning to Lydia with a voice fit for typhoid. 'Mumps, my angel. Oh, what if Terence . . . !'

'Breast-fed he'll not,' said Lydia. 'An' if he did it'd not do harm. He ought to get it over before 'is balls is down.'

'Lydia, leave the room!'

'What's matter?'

'Before Margaret! Anyhow, it isn't a phrase I can have in this house.'

'Ow', said Margaret again, 'I can't lift my head up. Can you shut the curtains?'

'It's *mumps*, darling,' said her mother again. 'Now don't worry. You'll just have to stay there a few days and have lovely cool drinks.'

'I want bacon,' she said, but when bacon came she couldn't deal with it. Lying flat, she prodded it back and forth with a fork and then let it drop down on the plate. She let the tea grow cold and got her fingers in the butter. 'Can't you prop me up?' she cried, but Lydia heaving at pillows had to stop and let her sink down again with wails. A doctor came and went. The day passed slowly. The sun mercifully moving away from the window at dinner time let her sleep. In the evening she said that she thought she must be very infectious and the note of relish made Mrs Marsh relax.

'It's only *mumps*,' said Lydia, 'an' both sides together so you'll soon be over it. You can't have it twice.'

'Have you had it, Lydia?'

'Don't know. Our Les an' all on them did. And me Mam. An' I looked after 'em.'

'How old were you?'

'I dunno. Thirteen.'

'Weren't you at school, Lydia?'

'I nivver bothered. Me Dad got it an' all.'

'Did you have to look after him, too?' Margaret whispered when her mother had returned to the cot.

'Nobody nivver looked after 'im.'

'Why?'

'Nobody went near 'im. 'E threw bottles at yer.'

'He sounds awful. What's balls going down.'

'Nivver mind.'

'Have I got them?'

'No.'

'Had your father?'

'Not 'alf.'

'I feel awful.'

'Here's aspirins. D'yer want the mirrer?'

Margaret, presented to herself, began to weep.

''Ere. Shurrup. You was meant to laugh.'

'Ss-ssh,' wept Margaret. 'You hurt my head. I'm changed.'

Her father came in and looked at her unsmiling. 'I have brought you some tablets,' he said.

'Exodus twenty-four twelve.'

'Hello?'

'I'm changed. Like snakes.'

'Snakes?'

'Shall we say a prayer?'

'It's all right.'

'It never goes amiss. Job thirty-three twenty-six.'

'His was boils. Mumps is nothing. Lydia said. Unless your balls haven't dropped. Maybe she meant *boils* haven't . . . ?' Mr Marsh went quickly from the room. 'Job's boils hadn't . . . ' said Margaret yawning, and shrieked. 'Yawning's terrible,' she said.

So were the next three days and she wondered if it was her rejection of the Scriptures.

The fourth day though was rather better and the fifth better still—she could feel the bumps beneath the swelling now and harped on their shape and tenderness. The next day she addressed to the insertion of ice-cream through her teeth and on the next was calling for braised steak and cabbage. Her mother, who had kept her distance because of Terence, now came in to read her a story, and her father paid her less attention. Terence she had not seen at all and had not missed and was told that it would be sensible to keep away from him for a while. 'Though the time when you were really infectious,' said her mother, 'was just before the swelling appeared. I do hope Binkie and Charles—I wonder if I should send Lydia to see . . . ?'

'Have Charles's . . . ?'
'That will do, Margaret.'

Two days later she was allowed to go out on the beach in the sun for twenty minutes and the next day for longer and by herself. She walked down by the sand-hills, then turned away from the sea. The sand-hills ran white behind her as she climbed them, wide shallow avalanches pouring like wide streams round the silver spikes of sharp grass. There was a change in the season. It took her some time to realise it, thinking for a bit that it was something to do with herself and the mumps. She noticed a different colour in the sunshine. Though it was still just as hot there was a clearness in the air and a deeper red to the geraniums and the dahlias in the flower-beds of the park which she had wandered into from the dunes. She walked about the park, considering.

The lobelias along the edges of the flower-beds seemed a deeper blue than last week and the sky slightly darker too. There were fewer people about. Holidays must be getting over. The thought of school beginning again drifted up and was quickly put away. She wandered over to the drinking fountain that stuck vulgarly up on its cement dais. She pressed its smooth knob. Water welled and bubbled roundly out of the hole. She knew that the drinking fountain was disgusting, germ-laden, corrupt, Leviticus five three—if he touch the uncleanness of man whatever uncleanness it be . . . They actually put their mouths over the spout, the day-trippers. They covered the spout with their lips. The horrors of the lips of trippers encompassed her Isaiah six five. I am a man of unclean lips and I live in the midst of a people of unclean lips . . .

Well, why? Why are trippers' lips bad? It's Mother's idea from Father from Isaiah. How did Isaiah know about spit? Jesus used spit. It was His own spit though. He used His own.

He didn't like the dumb man's spit. The dumb man wallowed foaming, Mark nine twenty.

Mother isn't clever. Neither's Father—she said so. In a way, she thought, Lydia is cleverer. She knows more things. Like about mumps. It's because she's been away. I wonder if she went to Cambridge?

She tried to imagine Cambridge and saw a grey place of avenues and, for some reason, sheep pens (no goats) all labelled for the clever people. She saw the people taken from the pens and set down in classrooms where they were looked at severely by grey men and all glared severely back. Some were sent in one direction, some in another and there was great seriousness and sternness like Jesus and Paul, and you couldn't see Lydia there. The water bubbled on.

'Hello,' said a voice.

The man, Charles, was beside her in a pale linen suit, swinging a walking-stick with a gold top. His moustache looked very soft like Robert Louis Stevenson's in the book at school. His face had the same kindness in it. His sloping shoulders looked just a bit soppy. Also like Robert Louis Stevenson. Yet extremely nice.

'And what are you thinking about?' asked Charles.

He got into step beside her as she moved off and she thought, I'm not going to say *Treasure Island*. It sounds like showing off. And he'll say, 'Does your father *allow* you to read *Treasure Island*,' and I'll say, 'It's school,' and then he'll go on and on and on with those awful questions.

'Dreaming over a water spout,' said Charles, 'a sprite.'

(It is going to be that daft game.)

'Like a thoughtful dryad.'

(I'm not asking what a dryad is, neither, she said silently in a Lydia voice.)

'A dryad,' he said, 'is a water fairy. I always thought it silly when I was your age to call anything to do with water dry! But it's a good way to remember it.'

(I bet he's a teacher.)

'Well, how are you?' he asked.

'All right. I've had mumps.'

'What—since you came to tea?'

'Yes. I'm out for just the second time.'

'You've been very quick. Sometimes mumps take much longer.'

'Have you had them?'

'Yes.'

'Oh, that's good.'

'It's a good thing to get over.'

'Yes. Had your . . . We were a bit afraid we'd given you them because I was terribly infectious, Mother says, when I came to tea.'

'I thought there was something.'

They walked on. She said, 'No. That wasn't the mumps.'

'Oh.'

'My being rude.'

'You weren't rude.'

'Mother said I was.'

'No. You weren't.'

'I didn't mean to be,' she said, 'but I meant to . . . '

'What?'

'I don't know.'

'Put me in my place?'

'I don't know what your place is.'

He sighed. 'Neither do I,' and slashed the walking-stick at a huge shaggy pink dahlia they were passing and snapped off its head.

'Oh.' She stopped in her tracks. She had not been so astonished and shocked since—something similar. Yes—since Mr Drinkwater had called the chaplain a fucking fool.

'What an *awful* thing to do!'

'Yes, isn't it?'

'Aren't you ash . . . You're awful!'

'Yes. That's right.'

'You must be—' the bland fat face of sweet Mr Drinkwater, and swashing slops of cobalt blue—'You're mad,' she said.

'That's right. They ought to put me in a Home. Why not come to the one I'm already in and have tea with Binkie and me again?'

'Now?'

'Why not?'

'All right.'

They stopped a moment on the kerb to cross to Dene Close and she looked up at him. He looked down at her and pulled a face, a terrible shocked look with eyes on stalks and pursed lips and a dropped jaw. He stuck his straw hat at an angle and danced a little jig. 'Mad Marmaduke,' he said. 'Well, that's better—I've not seen you laugh.' As they walked up the path to the rising sun she took his hand.

# 10.

In the half-dark Rosalie Frayling lay and waited for the call of the first bird. The room had never been really dark all night. Cool air had blown in through the open terrace windows, making some of the smaller pictures tap here and there. All through this long summer there had been no other sounds at night except occasionally when the trees across the lawns or over in the woods gave one toss and swished for a few moments. The past few weeks as it had grown even hotter there had been hardly a breeze of any kind, however, even at night, just long silence, long twilight, then slightly lighter twilight, then the first harsh chirrup, experimental, comic, the first long cry, then the dawn chorus, then the dawn.

From the high bed she could see the line of the pillow at her temple. Odd that her head, so small now with the scratty cap of hair, was still heavy enough to dent the pillow down. She lay straight as a plank, almost weightless, and watched the light gather round the huge windows which she refused to allow to be closed.

'You should have them shut at night,' the doctor said.

'I like the air.'

'What about the pictures?'

'There are no robbers.'

'Anyone could walk in. Straight off the beach and through the woods and across the park.'

'Nobody ever has,' she said. 'There has always been a notice on the bridge saying “Private.” I don’t believe we’ve ever had prowlers. I don’t know why.’

‘You might now,’ he said. ‘Times have changed.’

She thought of some shaggy tramp blundering in, breathing hard, falling over the wash-stand in the cruel pale hours before dawn, seeing her iron bed and her wide-eyed shadow on it. She said, ‘He’d be terrified.’

‘Not if he was after the pictures.’

‘There’s only the Renoir really,’ she said. ‘And it’s too high up. He’d hardly bring a ladder all the way.’

‘I should shut them though,’ the doctor said. ‘I should shut them. No point in inviting a disturbance.’

The first bird had finished chirping and in the pause before the chorus proper the light ran slowly along the left-hand side of the room, spreading from the direction of the conservatory behind her, bringing faint pattern to the heavy old brocade of the curtains not yet showing green, a shine to the fat belly of the water-jug on the wash-hand basin. With the great out-pouring of birdsong that followed, the sun catapulted up and sent immense momentary shadows springing from the trees on the lawns, making the picture-frames, row upon row, from dado to ceiling, blacken up, then suggest colour in blocks. The shielding curtains showed greyish green and a smell of grass and earth blew in. Rosalie moved her eyes upward towards the Renoir hung high on the cornice where she could see it. It was still just a patch in a heavy frame. Reassured even by its shape however she slept, waking only with the rumble and clatter of the night-nurse getting things ready to go off-duty—the wide swing of the door as she came in, the thud of her feet, the lift of the pillow, the breath taken to meet the pain of dropping her head forward to the feeding cup to sip at the tea.

‘Yer right. Yer grand. That’s right now.’ It was Effie from Hinderwell, kind and frowsty but far too familiar.

The moving-about, knocking-about noises in the room, the tossing of sheets, the cold horror of the bed pan. Effie's back politely turned at the window. Then the sun suddenly sprouting into the sky like midday, and still not eight o'clock.

'It's another,' said Effie. 'Another roaster.'

She must not groan as they eased her down. There's Joan there, too, now, sweet Joan with the fat mongol smile who had once been only a patient in the wards and now was a nurse. Or a servant—or a friend. One grew confused.

'Change yer sheets?' shouted Effie, splashing and sluicing behind the screen. 'No? Leave it for Nurse? All right then. More tea? No? Right-ho—see yer tonight.'

Mrs Frayling did not reply.

'Bye-bye,' said fat Joan, patting at her hand. 'Bye-bye, bye-bye.'

'Good-bye, Joan dear.'

Effie glinted and crashed out. 'Too grand for me. We'll condescend for fat Joan but seems we're too grand this morning for me.' Rosalie knew each thought. She closed her eyes and opened them only for the onslaught of Sister Booth at nine. Again she said nothing. Bread and butter was slid between her teeth, an egg soft-boiled expertly spoon-fed into her mouth, scraped off round her lips. More tea from the unspeakable spouted cup.

Booth did not speak either. Her huge bulk swung lightly about the room, her great sloped chest with its watch and military medals which rested there rather than hung, her big truculent face above, coarse black hairs along the upper lip, the speaking wet brown eyes, the clamped jaw. Booth and Rosalie closed with one another for a new day in the mutual professional duet which masked both disgust and love.

Listening to the slap and heave of Booth with sheets and counterpane, the sharp directions to fat Joan, the brisk pouring of water, the squeeze and shake of the face-flannel and the clink of the toothbrush being rinsed in the glass, Rosalie marvelled at the death of an old and different affection—passion. And love and passion for men, for example. She remembered such things now—desperation, longing—only in the image of herself suffering it. The 'affaire,' she thought, all it is now is myself, vague, distracted, the children looking bewildered, husband pointedly unnoticing, the object of all adoration now hazier than myself longing for it. For him. The army Captain, 1917. Recovering from France. One of the convalescents they'd looked after when the house had been made like all the other suitable houses round about into a convalescent home.

He had sat on the terrace looking over the park and the tennis court, day after day after day in a summer not unlike this one. He had sat perfectly still. In a dressing-gown. She remembered all of a sudden the fringe on the silk tie of the dressing-gown—gold thread like a book-mark on a lectern. Or a mediaeval moustache. He had sat looking at the broad lawns, watching the peacefulness of the gardeners and other quiet wounded men in groups under the trees. All their faces and his particularly had looked as if they were listening to other things and seeing another landscape.

She had begun by smiling at him each morning as she walked by with the day's basket of house-flowers she had taken from the cutting garden near the black shed—stiff, long gladioli, airier spikes of delphinium. Though he had never even lifted his head, or smiled back, soon she found that she had stopped beside him and said this and that about the day. Soon she had discovered that most days were important only because of this meeting, and that at length she was sitting on the terrace beside him without the flowers, but with sewing. Then that the sewing lay for an hour or for two hours in her lap. Later she sat beside him with nothing in her lap and with no excuse and between them there had been such knowledge that she had felt lost and diminished the moment she had moved away from him.

One day, she remembered, arriving on the terrace and finding him not there she had had to cling to the stone jar of geraniums at the top of the steps, had said to the little marble statue from Florence of the boy eating grapes, 'He's gone. He's dead.' When they had wheeled him round the corner at the same minute and then left him with her she had said in terror, 'One day you'll go away,' and he had looked at her and held her hand.

She tried hard now—Booth was haranguing Effie. Something about Lysol—to remember, and saw a high cheekboned face, young skin, large and very tired blue eyes, a droop of brown moustache, a long, fine, bony hand along the arm of the metal wheel-chair.

A bouncy bossy rosy wife arrived soon after. Her laugh had clattered over the terrace, shrieked about the lawns and into the wood. She had been called Nancy. He had been called . . .

But she could not remember his name.

The hell of the blowsy August, after the wife had taken him home, remained; and the memory of herself, drifting about, forgetting to keep appointments, bursting once into painful tears at breakfast, running off, down to the beach, walking there all day, until it was dark, by the sea, raging and cursing at the words not said, the love not given. The time—the event, the 'affaire'—remained now in memories of the puzzled faces of Charles and Binkie. 'Mama—are you ill or something?'

Edward at the other end of the table, moving forks about, looking grave.

And on holiday—a holiday that had passed like sick sleep at Scarborough, 'I am lonely with everyone,' she had thought. 'It will always be the same. There is nobody but him.'

Then one day, at home again in September, she had noticed

the apples in the kitchen garden. With the dark blue sky behind, the multitudinous and polished, crimson hard apples among frills of leaf. Beautiful, she had thought and smiled at them. The bird was flown.

And now she had even forgotten his name.

The waste of emotion. The pointlessness of it. Remembering poor old Edward was better, though even so she could not really, when she put her mind to it, remember Edward's face.

She couldn't remember his proposal at all—again it was only herself she remembered, coming through the open windows—these windows presumably, since this had been the drawing-room—and her mother, small, curvaceous, corsetted and frisky, writing ten to the dozen at the little davenport. The desk—lovely desk—with the sloping lid, smiling as she wrote.

'Darling'—one hand up in the air, sensing Rosalie at the window—'Catching the post. Won't be a minute. Writing to—oh, such a scream!'

'I'm going to marry Edward.'

The pen rushing on. Then flung down. The hour-glass figure turning, arms in air, the bright eyes, little black eyebrows. 'Rosalie! Rosalie! Oh, oh!'

'He's just asked me. I've said yes.'

'Rosalie, Rosalie!'

'Is it all right?' she had said. She had been seventeen.

Booth bore down on her with a big ivory hair-brush and a metal bowl.

'Leave my hair, Booth. It can wait.'

'You'll feel better if it's done.'

'There's not enough to show a profit.'

At seventeen, standing in the window her hair had been a heap of heavy, dark orange silk, looped and coiled and pinned and twisted into a final, fat silk plait. Heavy and hot. Rather horrible really, she thought now. Like weeds growing. Animals, she thought, as Booth scrubbed about, are so much more beautiful, covered matt with silk or fuzz. Men like great weedy trails of hair—I wonder why? We all cut it off later. The wounded Captain never saw me with great heaps of hair. Edward had, but had Edward liked her hair?

She couldn't remember.

Charles had. When he was what—six? He used to sit and watch her brushing it. He said he liked to see the spikes come through. 'Like hedgehogs.'

Binkie never gave a thought to hair—her mother's or her own or anybody's. She never looked at jewellery and she didn't care a blow for clothes. Or pictures. All Economics with her, Girton, those terrible gaunt women. Political Theory.

What sort of daughters would I have had with the wounded Captain?

The feeding cup was approaching in Booth's white hands above her head like a moon. It descends. I am like a cat. I am covered in black silk. I see the saucer descend. Shall I purr?

Shall I purr at Booth? Her eyes would bulge out like great melting sweets, sucky sweets. Sweeties, mint bullets. Are there mint bullets any more? Mint Imperials? Mints of Empire? It would be worth purring to see Booth's fat face.

I shall not cry. I shall not cry out.

She drank soup out of the abomination, Booth expertly mopping up. She swallowed pills. Booth sat by her with the *Daily Telegraph.* She soon stopped listening to Booth and slept.

She slept till four—she knew that it was four, because four o'clock in the summer was the time when the Renoir was lit by the sun, and when the child's face shone best. It was a young child with red rather pouted-out lips craning forward to look at something out of the picture, her eyes big and awake and content and her head as round as a football. She had yellow hair. She sat—though it was only a small picture—a head with hardly an inch around it—in a yellow and pink garden in summer. The head looked earnestly across at something and very much at its ease. Edward had bought the Renoir. In Paris when he was young.

'But he's so old,' the hour-glass figure had cried, with the pen tossed out of its hand, then covering her mouth with the other one. 'Oh—darling—oh! I'm sorry. But should you?'

'I've said yes.'

'But you're seventeen. He's the very first . . . My dear, it's not . . . It's nothing to do with me, but . . . '

A mother so far ahead of her time, refusing to dictate, determined to let her children choose for themselves, determined to let Rosalie make decisions she said girls had been deprived of since the flood. I wanted to be told NO, Rosalie thought now. I suppose that's why I was such a martinet with my own.

That's why I never let them alone. I dictated to Binkie and look at her—just like a man. Like a sergeant-major. Not a trace of femininity in her. She's worse than Booth. Charles I harangued. He just stood there and listened. I knew that everybody was saying that I ran him. But I couldn't stop. I stopped that marriage. I knew I was doing it—hurting him nearly to death—and I still went on. That self-conscious creature with the bosoms who never stopped blushing, Elinor the dustman's daughter. Goodness knows where the mother came from. We had been good to her—and there. She caught him—or thought she had. Edward could not have borne Charles to marry someone with—well, no background at all. Even though he was dead by then.

I stopped that. I'm not sorry. I'm not sure that Charles ever forgave me. He never comes near me. I shan't ever know.

Neither of them comes near me, though Binkie calls. Like some parish visitor. She doesn't come near me.

Why couldn't she have said, 'I forbid it! I FORBID IT, ROSALIE. He is so old?' Flinging the pen down—right across the room, thumping the davenport (where is the davenport? It was a lovely piece that desk—a *delectable* piece Edward always called it), 'Rosalie, I forbid you to marry Edward Frayling. He is FAR TOO OLD.'

I should not have had the Renoir then. I should not have been able to stay in this house. We could not have kept any of it if I had not married Edward Frayling. I should be in a Home now. It would have been some horrible nursing home, not my own house. I shouldn't have been able to turn the house over to the poor mental patients. I should have been a mental case myself by this time if I'd waited and married someone like the wounded Captain. Giles? Miles? Name gone.

They said I grew very odd. I'd have grown odder. Married to Edward I could keep the oddness under—talk to left and right at dinner parties, open things and cut ribbons, receive bouquets, always impressive, correct, distant, taking soup round in the worst times at the Works. After the War.

'It's time you went outside.'

'Not today, Booth.' (She makes it sound like a dog.)

'There's a bit of a breeze now.'

'I don't see how you can know, Booth. You've not been out yourself.'

'There's a tree top moving over in the woods—you can see the top of it swaying about.'

Perhaps somebody is climbing it. I used to climb the trees. Charles did. (Basil? Nigel?)

Booth rattled the newspaper and sniffed and Rosalie heard her scratching herself. 'I've made up the carriage,' she said after a while in a voice to cover herself. Rosalie did not believe it. The carriage squeaked and vibrated as it was prepared and she had heard no noise. Booth did not mind missing the perambulation into the air. Like a lazy nannie with a docile child she liked being comfortable indoors. In fact it was almost worth enduring the outing to get Booth's great reluctant shape heaving about the gardens.

Almost, but not quite. The shift from bed to carriage was getting more painful now each day, leaving her limp, unable to talk for most of the afternoon, trying all the time she lay looking at the sky not to think of the terrible return journey, and giving her hallucinations more extraordinary than dreams. Last week she had seen the Renoir head appear in the full light of day over the side of the carriage in the kitchen garden when she had sent Booth round the back of the black shed so that she need not hear the knitting needles. The head with bright hair, luminous with health, round as a football, wide eyed and strong had examined her with confidence like recognition—and then was gone, leaving just the pattern of the apple tree in its place all lichen and leaf-curl against the harsh blue sky, and not one red fruit.

'Very well then,' said Booth contentedly, 'but we'll have to go tomorrow. You must get your fresh air.' She lay back creaking in the easy chair. There was the sound of the knitting bag coming out and then the clicking and the raising high of Booth's arm pulling out wool. When Booth's arm rose, the smell of Booth was strong. You could see the damp patches under Booth's arm sometimes in the afternoon; sometimes in this weather even before lunch. I expect I smell, too, thought Rosalie. How can I know?

A plump figure moved about the room somewhere and Booth was gone. 'Hello,' Rosalie called. I must have been asleep. 'Who's there?' Someone had wandered in from the conservatory behind and past her.

'Drinkwater.'

She felt him moving about, walking up and down the far end of the huge room, and a little tapping noise.

'What's the tapping?'

'I'm looking at Lake Maggiore.'

'Why should it cause you to tap?'

He drifted up to her with the silver pencil in his mouth and rattled it over his teeth. 'Magnificent,' he said.

'Your teeth?'

'Lake Maggiore. One of my best.'

'It's not one of yours. It's a William Leighton Leitch.'

'Ah. I've lost Mount Parnassus.' He wandered off.

'Behind the washstand.'

'Ah. Yes. Mount Parnassus on the Road between Livadia and Delphi.'

'Yes. John Robert Cozens.'

She saw his back droop. He was wearing a navy-blue gaberdine macintosh today, belted in like a schoolboy, and if I could see the feet, she thought, I'd not be surprised by wellingtons.

'Mount Parnassus *was* one of mine.'

'Not that one. That one is John Robert Cozens.'

'I've been to Delphi, you know. Painted there. Summer of eighty–four.'

'Cozens was dead in eighty-four. Probably in seventeen eighty-four.'

Together they looked at their memory of Mount Olympus on the road near Delphi—the filmy, sunny slope above the dapple of the landscape of trees and shepherds and a haunch of a great ruin, leaning, sun-hardened. Rosalie saw the picture, straining after it as she had done for the name of the wounded Captain, catching only the line of shadow she remembered on the lowest peaks, the splash of sun behind the nearest scrub. 'Hawthorns,' she said, 'I always thought they were probably hawthorns. They're certainly not olives.'

'No, no. Certainly not,' said Mr Drinkwater, peering forward.

'I wonder if he was only in the Lake District all the time?'

'No, no. We were at Delphi. I was there with Lear you know. Painting holiday. Summer of forty-nine. Never much cared for the Lakes.'

'*Forty*-nine?' By turning her eyes and then holding her breath and straining her neck she turned her head a very little towards the picture and saw that Drinkwater was peering with satisfaction at the one next to it. 'You're not even looking at it,' she said. 'That's William Collins. Trees in Windsor Park.'

'Certainly not,' said Drinkwater growing flushed, 'I've never been to Windsor Park in my life. Worse than the Lake District.' His outraged face swelled like a cat's above the macintosh which was buttoned to the chin, his beard fluffing out all round. He wore as usual his panama hat. She smiled at him with love.

'Do you need that macintosh today, Edwin?'

He looked at it surprised. 'Never know in the Lake District,' he said. 'Rain can start any time. Terrible for painting. Light changing minute by minute. Never go a step in the Lakes without a mac. Take my advice.'

'I will. Are you painting today?'

'No. No. Too many people about. That nurse in Ward B—the whatsnames—aphrodisiacs . . . '

'Euphorics.'

'Ha—that's the fellers—Ward B. She has them out in droves.'

'Do they bother you. I'll have them stopped.'

'No. No. I chuck a few things at them. They go off.'

'Don't hurt them. What do you chuck?'

'Oh—stones. Grenades. Anything about me. That girl's been here again you know.'

'What girl?'

'That girl I told you about. Fond of snakes. Rolls about and talks. Child.'

'A child? By herself? In the grounds?'

'Yes. Healthy. Rosy thing. Serious. About seven. Looks at you.'

Rosalie eased her head back into its hollow. Soon Booth would be back. The talcum powder, the dressings. She had a way of easing the leaden pressure of the sheets. I only keep Booth, she thought, because she has a gift for preventing bedsores. 'No bedsores with Booth,' she says. She had been a famous VAD in the hospitals of the Somme turning and pummelling and heaving and thumping soldiers who had often wept and asked to be left to die in peace. Her medals proved it. She spoke heartily about it all, often.

The sort of woman, thought Rosalie, I would once not have had in my drawing room. No more than the other one—Charles's.

Drinkwater had wandered to the window and was stepping out. 'Stay for tea,' called Rosalie. 'Booth will be back soon.'

'Tea's over,' said Drinkwater. Suddenly rational he looked at her amazed. 'You're losing your grip, Rosalie. Tea's over. It's past supper. There's your tray. Empty.'

'I must have been asleep again,' she said. 'I suppose I should have let her take me out this afternoon. Then I'd have slept tonight.'

'You can't have slept tonight. Tonight isn't here yet. Not quite.'

Looking up at the Renoir she saw that this was true for the sun was off it—was off the whole room again. There was only a sense of it far outside the windows, still slinking at the edge of the lawns, making a gold edge to the flower borders lighting the red walls of the kitchen garden to an orange-rose. 'I shan't see that again, I expect,' she thought. Looking hard at the shadowed Renoir she said, 'I wonder if that child was a ghost?'

Drinkwater had moved off.

Still looking at the picture or what she could see of it, Rosalie thought about him and the pleasure he gave her. Drinkwater and fat mongol Joan, she thought. Only the mad now seem to do. It's only the mad I seem to understand at all. I should like to talk to Charles again sometimes—he had a nonsensical streak. We used to talk rubbish together when he was little. I expect he's forgotten about it all now. I'll leave the Renoir to Drinkwater in case they throw him out when I am dead. Find he can't pay. I shan't leave it to Charles. He can have all the dying stags—no, I'll be kind. He can have the Lake District olives.

'I'll leave Binkie the dying stags,' she thought, 'and the dead pheasants with the glass eyes and the overblown roses. She can sell them if she wants. I'll leave all the good landscapes to Drinkwater.' She wondered a little if Binkie—or even Booth—might know something about the wounded Captain.

The light had nearly gone. It faded slowly, running down the right-hand side of the water glass and the other flank of the belly of the water jug. Outside a bird twittered now and then and at length was quiet. The door opened and Effie came in with a lamp. Then Effie—the bed pan, the talcum, the horror. Pills. Effie passed her the prayer book while she went away behind the screen, to swish about with buckets, and took the book away again—it had stayed unopened—and put it on the bedside table and the lamp beside it.

'Anything you want, dear?'

Rosalie said nothing.

'All right then, duckie?'

'I am Mrs Frayling.'

'Sorry. All right then, Mrs Frayling?' (There'll be a stop to all this one day, you wait. It's another war we want.)

'No thank you, nurse. Yes—take the light. Goodnight.'

'Goodnight, Mrs Frayling' (unappeased).

The light gone, in the half-dark, Rosalie Frayling lay and waited for the call of the first bird.

# 11.

As Charles opened the sun-ray door there was an outlandish crash and Binkie dropped all the scones out of the oven. The tray they were on and the iron grid the tray had been on and the scones and massive Binkie went rolling about the shiny linoleum and Binkie moaned and yelled. The big body and the scattered food and metal made queer groups in the breezy cheerful kitchen and Margaret looked down at Binkie's face with round eyes.

'Dear me,' said Charles. 'Too hot.'

'I slipped.' Binkie the steady instructress of the other tea time glared furiously at Margaret from under the kitchen table. 'Why don't you laugh?' she said, hauling herself up. 'It's comic. That's all it is. Comic. Don't you read the Comic Cuts? Don't look so disappointed. Go into the garden.'

Charles and Margaret went out of thc back door and sat on a bench in the garden silently, with a sense of shame.

'I think I'll go home now,' said Margaret in a minute.

'No—no,' said Charles. 'Wait. It'll be all right. You'll see.'

Binkie marched out bearing a jug.

'Good,' said Charles. 'Lemonade.'

Binkie threw the contents of the jug over some crackling dry azaleas and went back into the house.

'Apparently not,' he said.

They sat on and at length a kitchen window opened and Binkie could be heard splashing about.

'Margaret has had mumps,' Charles called. 'Could we have a scone?'

The tiny garden was one of a crescent of little gardens divided from one another by cheap chestnut fencing. The grass patch and flower border in it were weedless, trimmed at the edges like cloth. The flowers stood at measured intervals unlike the gardens on either side where there seemed to be things untidy on trellises and sheds with pigeons, washing lines and brittle plate-headed sunflowers looking like hanged men in the heat. In the middle of Charles's and Binkie's grass plot stood a small plinth with a marble boy on it eating grapes. The marble looked silky, creamy, more alive than the flowers and as odd standing on the square of grass as Binkie had done rolling so curiously on the linoleum. Charles said, 'You look worried. Shall I get a book and read to you?'

'No. I think I'll go now. I'd better.'

'Binkie's knee had given way, that's all. She thinks she's got something wrong with her. It's in the family—a thing you don't mention. She hates to show fright. She's upset that we saw her. She'll be all right soon—look.'

And Binkie now came out on the lawn with a plate of buttered scones and a tea-pot. She put them on a garden table and went back for cups and milk jug and jam. She pulled up a deck chair for herself, sat down and poured the tea.

'So—mumps?' she said ferociously.

'Yes. I was getting it last time I was here.'

'Just as well we'd all had it.'

'I was feeling a bit funny that day.'

'Funny?' She digested the information while demolishing scones heavy with gouts of jam and began to look more cheerful. 'Home made,' she said of the jam. 'Have some. Don't look so disappointed.'

'I'm not . . . ' But Margaret realised that she was. And shaken up. Binkie at the first meeting had filled her with strength—someone who knew exactly what she was about and caring for nobody's opinion in heaven or earth. Popes and potentates would watch their step just like with Father and the Saints. Binkie had told you what to do, but you felt that she told you things for their own sake and not because you would get some prize for it one day in the hereafter. You had felt that Binkie had only the faintest picture of the Holy City and perhaps no great opinion of it anyway, with its ornate gates and angels Revelation twenty-one twelve. She would think about truth very coolly and in her own time.

Yet Binkie today had been in rout, collapsed and discountenanced and not special at all. Margaret had not known that her admiration for Binkie had been so comforting until it was gone.

There was something else the matter, too. Eating a jammy scone Margaret thought, 'He might have helped with the tea things and to pick her up off the floor. Even Father would have carried the deck chair for her.'

Looking up at the peaceful face of Charles she thought, 'I don't like him very much. He's soppy.'

'How's your mother?' asked Binkie.

'All right.'

'Has the baby had mumps?'

'No. He's breast-fed.'

There was a bit of a silence. 'I hope nobody else at home gets them,' Charles said.

'Well, Elinor won't,' said Binkie. 'She had them when she was four. When you did.'

'Did she?'

'Yes—don't you remember? With Miss Pannell. We all did.'

'I don't remember.'

'Well, you were only four.'

'What's Miss-panel?' asked Margaret.

'She was our governess,' said Charles. 'We three shared a governess.'

'What's a governess?'

'A private teacher.'

'Just for three?'

'Yes.'

'What a tiny little school.'

'Miss Pannell lived in our house. Your mother lived near us—we all lived in Eastkirk then and we shared her. Shared Miss Pannell.'

'Was it very tiny?'

'The little school?'

She had a picture of a doll's house and of Charles and Binkie and her mother all crammed in with a witch, as large as they were now but with funny unlined faces.

'It was big,' said Charles laughing: 'Immense.'

The doll's house spread, the figures shrank to pins.

'It had miles of sloping grass all round it,' said Charles, 'and woods and huge kitchen gardens, with rows of fresh vegetables, and eight gardeners all in the same coloured overalls. Sandy overalls.'

'There was a terrace,' said Binkie suddenly, 'with stone jars. That boy used to stand on it.' She pointed to the marble figure. 'We used to have our lessons on the terrace sometimes. And sometimes in the conservatory.'

'What's a conservatory?'

'A huge greenhouse. It had a vine in it—with hundreds and hundreds of bunches of grapes. It was heated by a massive stone stove. Like a steam-engine. There was a man who did nothing in the winter but shovel. I wonder what he did in the summer?'

'Kept the post office,' said Charles, 'or wait a minute—no. It was his wife who kept the post office and he did some sort of public—yes that's it, he took on the council dust carts in summer. Always kept the lamps and brasses shining on the dust cart—d'you remember. Well—wasn't it Ellie's—?'

'And in the conservatory for lessons,' said Binkie. 'We all used to sit in big basket chairs.'

'With holes woven in the arms to take a glass. You could drop sweets in.'

'It got hot in there,' said Binkie. 'Sometimes Miss Pannell fell asleep. She had a feather fan.'

'Was Mother—what was Mother like then?'

Binkie said, 'Quiet.'

Charles said, 'Exactly the same.'

'As now? She couldn't be. She'd be lower down. Nearer the ground.'

'Well so were we.'

The brother and sister sat slowly munching. Charles pressed a finger into first one and then another crumb on his plate and put the collection in his mouth when it threatened to scatter again. Binkie stared hard at the azalea with its dwarf burnt-up leaves and undersized withered flowers. It occurred to Margaret that it wasn't being much fun today, and no jokes at all. Miserable really. She began to think of Lydia then, remembering that Lydia was so moody these days, thought instead of the painter at the mansion.

'I saw a lot of people like flowers. Walking in a crocodile,' she said in the sleepy silence.

'Flowers in a crocodile?' Charles's attempt to revive the jocular tea-party of the week before was like an invalid heaving bricks. The hope of nonsense hung very slightly in the air and then departed. They sat on.

You could say anything today, Margaret thought. About Jesus and broken hearts. About Lydia. About Lydia's corsets. About Lydia's man, even. They wouldn't notice. They are a funny pair.

'Did my mother like you very much when she was young?' she asked.

It was amazing how it woke them up.

They both turned and stared at her astounded. She thought, well then. I've done it. Even more than with Jesus's heart. I've really shattered them. I wonder whatever I've said.

'Well I . . . ' Binkie looked hard at the marble statue.

'Why do you ask?' Charles had a wonderfully compassionate look.

'Well—I just can't see her . . . '

Binkie said haughtily in the direction of the grape-eating boy, 'I think they were very grateful . . . ' Charles frowned.

'Who?'

'Her people. Your mother's people.'

'Her people? Was she a queen?' She knew at once that this was silly. Of course her mother hadn't been a queen. Her mother's father had been 'Something to Do with the Council.' Queens and Councils though—perhaps a Council was something she didn't understand and her mother had in fact been regal in some way. She did always look very stately and sweet. She was different—you could see in Turner Street—from the others there. It was something about her clothes. They were loose and traily. She never looked a lump like—well even this Binkie. How very kind of her it had been to share Miss Pannell with the brother and sister and visit them at their home and sit with them in the greenhouse. Her people must have been glad that she had got to know some ordinary children.

'It must have been lovely for you to know my mother,' she said. The two faces looked stony.

At last Binkie said they had all been very good friends and it was time Margaret went home.

'I'll take you to the end of your road,' said Charles and they walked in silence. As they parted she shook hands with him and curtsied as her mother liked her to do, though nobody else at school or Turner Street did. Charles from his great height drooped down and said, 'A great pleasure to see you again.' Yet there was still something non-plussed about him.

'By the way,' he said, 'it was, of course.'

'What?'

'Lovely for us. To know your mother. Have her about.'

'Oh I'm sure,' said Margaret kindly.

Doing the pavement crack game down Seaview Villas she thought, 'I seem to have absolutely knocked them over. Binkie was knocked over from the start. Bowling about on the lino. Bowled over. I wonder why? I wonder why I feel I've won something?

'Victorious,' she thought, 'I feel victorious.'

# 12.

It was brawn and shape for high tea. The brawn was glossy and the shape was matt. Otherwise there was little between them and they were both pale brown. There were three tomatoes, bread and butter, a flabby lettuce and two bottles of HP and Heinz tomato sauce, tea and a plate of cream crackers. The dining room was nearly filled by the table which had legs like black barley sugar as thick as four thighs. There were of course no pictures on the cream walls, a sideboard had only a fruit bowl on it containing two black bananas. Outside the window was a yard with a grey mop upended leaning against a wall and beyond this the vegetable patch. A big varnished clock ticked like mad on the mantelpiece and a huge cartwheel of metal hung down from above the table, a light bulb suspended within and a no-coloured silk shade hugely draping it all with hideous pleats. The brawn was slithery on the tongue. Elinor Marsh chased it abstractedly about her plate and Marsh munched it loosely at the other end of the table, looking out over her head at the drooped head of the yard mop.

Next he chewed lettuce. Margaret slipped into her place.

'You are *very* late.'

'I've been out to tea.'

'Without asking!' Elinor came to life in a moment. 'To tea? Where? Darling?'

'To the brother and the sister's.'

Her father stopped eating and said, 'The Saints?'

'No. To Mummy's friends. The brother and the sister.'

'Did your mother know? Did you know this, Elinor? Who are these—?'

'They're just where Margaret and I went the other day.'

'I thought you went to old Mrs . . . ?'

'No.'

'Who is this brother and sister?'

'Well—the Fraylings. Binkie. The ones who came back . . . '

There was a heavy silence while Margaret tried to eat brawn. The noise of her fork vied with the clatter of the clock.

'We shall go on to the shape,' said Marsh. 'You will have to catch up.'

Margaret considered going on to the shape and thought blindingly this time of Drinkwater. What sort of shape? Remembering the first lovely tea-party which she had ruined she remembered the spring in the atmosphere at its beginning, and how her mother's face had lit up, and Charles's. They would both have been whizzing now, she thought. All kinds of ideas whizzing. 'What kind of shape would you care to take, Elinor?'

'I always change in the afternoon.'

'I have stopped changing and I have given up maids.'

'What is your opinion of giving up maids?'

'What do you think of giving up maids, Mr Drinkwater?'

'Oh many a maid, my dear Margaret, many a mop.'

'Many a mop,' said Charles, 'and many a mow.'

'But what is a mow?' asked Mother.

'A *barley* mow,' said Charles.

'A *Charley* mow,' said Binkie.

'Chase me Charley,' sang Lydia.

'Chase me Charley.'

'Find the barley . . . '

'Up the leg of me drawers,' sang Mr Marsh.

'The leg of me DRAWERS,' sang Lydia resoundingly to the accompaniment of brass and the ladies with sheet music and the soft sigh of the sea and the jingle of the bag and the rocking of the big black pram with the sleeping child in it—lucky as in a manger just breathing and sleeping and being fed and everyone adoring, adoring Matthew two two—

> 'Bringing in the sheaves,' sang Lydia.
> 'Bringing in the sheaves,
> We shall find the barley
> Bringing in the sheaves.'

Margaret blinked herself back into the dining room, splattered brown sauce all over her lettuce, looked at it with revulsion and said, 'We had scones with jam—home-made.' She looked at her mother and was astonished to find that she was crying. While she, Margaret, had been thinking of shapes, a quarrel had sprung up.

'It was the best time of my life. That's what it was if you want to know.'

'Before the child!' her father shouted.

'I don't care. I had a better time when I was eight than Margaret has ever had. She shall hear if I want. She *shall* hear.'

'You were in sin.'

'Rubbish.'

'Champagne. Vice. People you should have had nothing to do with. As if life was to do—education of the soul—to do with having a good time. Parties! Screaming and frolicking! *Garden* parties. Psalm seventy-eight nineteen. A table in the wilderness.'

'They were my friends.'

'They were not—and are not if I know anything—serious people. I forbid you to see them. And I forbid Margaret.'

'You can't forbid me, Kenneth.'

'Esphesians five twenty-two.'

'Oh for goodness sake!'

'It is goodness I am talking about.'

'I'm sick of it. I'm sick of it. I'm sick of goodness. I'm sick of you.' She ran out and slammed the door, then came back and held it very wide so that she could be heard along in the kitchen as well.

'And what about Lydia?'

'Whatever has Lydia to do with your Fraylings? I got you away from the works of the devil and I will get her away too, God willing. They could ruin you still as Lydia will be ruined without help. That is the only connection between you and Lydia. Lydia was sent me.'

'Why weren't the Fraylings sent then? Sent to me? When I was five.'

'They were. They were sent to be withstood.'

'At five! For heaven's sake, Kenneth. That happy place. If you'd known it. If only you had been sent the Fraylings. If you'd had the luck to be with easy-going . . . oh, instead of all this . . . '

'This what?'

'This hell-fire rubbish.'

She fled. Margaret, forgetting shape, went after her up the stairs but then grew shy and ran into her own bedroom where she bumped about trying not to hear the sobs from her mother's room across the landing. She opened and shut drawers noisily instead of calling out, and soon her mother appeared clutching and rocking the baby. She squeezed it up to her and kissed it and gulped and like a heavy pea-pod or a feather-tailed fish in its long shawl it slept unconcernedly on.

Margaret said, 'I heard about Miss Pannell.'

Elinor rocked about. 'Miss Pannell,' she said, 'Miss Pannell. They've just come back to live here, Margaret. After years. I knew them when I was five.'

'Charles was four. Four when he got mumps.'

'Yes.' She sobbed and then said, 'Miss Pannell used to go to sleep.'

'Yes—in the observatory.'

'Conservatory.'

'In the basket chair. With holes woven in the arms for glasses of lemonade.'

Grateful and surprised Elinor looked up. 'Yes,' she said. 'Yes, I'd forgotten the holes.' She fumbled about under the baby and brought out a handkerchief from somewhere. Margaret thought I wish she weren't a heap of boneless clothes. She needn't sit like a potato. She's wearing those awful green stockings again. Then in guilt she put her arm round her mother on the bed and rested her head against her. After a while her mother said in the queer Frayling way, '*Can* one weave holes?,' and Margaret said at once, 'Yes. If you can nets. Nets are just holes.' They looked at each other and Mrs Marsh's face edged towards a smile.

'They put sweets in them,' said Margaret.

'Charles put sweets in them,' Elinor corrected. 'He put caterpillars in them too. And worms. There were yells when she woke up. He was *very* naughty.'

'Did you love him?'

Mrs Marsh had grown deaf and rocked away at Terence. 'Mrs Frayling used to come sweeping in,' she said. 'Like a tall angel. Wonderful. Oh, her hair! So beautiful. I adored her. Her dresses!'

'What sort of dresses?' She squirmed with wickedness Peter three three.

'Muslin. Muslin. Sometimes crêpe—but lovely muslin in the mornings. She was very slender. She had lovely long fingers all rings—pale rings. And pearls. Pearly things. She collected pictures. She used to make us look at them for hours. Charles and Binkie were bored stiff.'

'Were you bored stiff?'

'Never. Never. Never.'

'Where did all of it go? The place and everything?'

'Nowhere. It's all still there. I am not, that's all. Mrs Frayling may be dead by now of course—I heard that she became very ill oh, years ago. She seemed much older than she was—always walked with a stick. Charles and Binkie went away over ten years ago—they've only just come back.'

'Why did they come back?'

'I don't know. I only heard a little while ago they had come back and were living in that . . . It was a shock, that house. You see, Charles and Binkie . . . '

'They're all right.' Margaret felt very bossy and in control as her mother started to weep again. 'They're all right. They're fine. But that's all. They're a bit boring though, aren't they?'

'Yes,' said Elinor. 'Yes. That's right. You're quite right. That's just what they are. They're so changed they've nearly gone. It's very silly to get haunted by the past and I think, darling—' and her voice became tender and self-conscious and the real coversation, the first ever, had passed. 'I think, darling, that we won't bother with the silly Fraylings any more.'

'Run off, dear,' she pushed Margaret gently away. 'Run down and say a nice goodnight to your father.'

Downstairs, directly beneath them, Marsh scraped his shape plate absolutely clean and then ate three cream crackers, hardly taking his glance for a moment off the back yard. He sat very quiet after the cream crackers, so that Lydia coming in to take the dirty plates was surprised to see anybody still there. ''Ullo,' she said. 'Well I never!' and then waited to be told that this was not the way she should speak.

But he said nothing and when she came close to the table and stretched near him to take the over-ripe bananas out of the sideboard dish behind his shoulder he did not shrink. 'Best get rid of these nasty things,' she said. When she leaned in front of him with the other hand to take his plate he took hold of her wrist.

She looked down at him. He still looked out of the window, steadily at the grizzled mop, and the clock ticked. Along the corridor she could hear the kitchen tap running for she had not shut the door behind her and had expected to be going straight back to the sink.

'What's this then?' she said. Looking at the top of his head she took a step nearer so that her round hip touched his shoulder.

He let go her wrist and slid his hand up her arm, up under the sleeve of her shiny dress. His fingers began to squeeze her arm hard. She looked down at the soft rather thin hair and the other hand, white and precise, which was lying on a dinner napkin.

The nails were pink and neat and clean. He held the napkin ring very tight. He looked up. She thought, 'False teeth, poor sod,' but tears came into her eyes and she leaned up closer. 'Eh?' she said.

'I want you,' he said.

Margaret when she passed the open door on her way down from upstairs saw her father's small, irreproachable, bank manager's hands moving desperately, quickly, darting, rubbing about over Lydia's big silk back.

# 13.

I can't go round there.

That's the misery.

When I was five, or ten, or fifteen, or eighteen I would have run round to them any time. Without warning. I ran out of the house—through the shop perhaps to tell my mother, down the road and then down the lane and in through the lodge gates. I waved to them in the lodge and then I walked down the drive and round the side of the conservatory and put my head round and if he wasn't there I just wandered into the gardens or down in the wood or back into the house through the side door and up the back stairs and into the attics or the library or the kitchens.

Anyone who saw me said, 'Hello, Ellie, looking for Charles?' They never said, 'Looking for Binkie?' From the beginning it was Charles and Ellie. Sometimes when I seemed to have looked everywhere and started home again I'd meet him coming back because he'd been down to the village looking for me. We'd sit down in the drive by the rhododendrons. In spring there was about a mile of daffodils—all down the drive and in little drifts across the park. He was so thin—so thin. 'They'll never rear him,' they used to say in the kitchen. 'No marrer in 'im.' At first I was plump as a plum. On wet days we went together into the library and sat on the window seat. I read a lot more than he did. He played. Soldiers, soldiers, soldiers because he wanted to command empires. His empires always won. But I didn't care. He commanded. 'Remove your *troops*,' he used to shout—his voice was very queer and high and stuttery and the words fell out like explosions. 'Pay me tribute. Five thousand gazoos.' I grew thin.

Binkie was never there. Goodness knows where Binkie was those afternoons. Tennis and piano and elocution and all the right things. Dancing class. She was terrible on the piano. Great thunderous bangs. Charles knew how awful she was as well as I did but we never spoke of it. I read the big leather books on the shelves in the library and he moved the troops across the floor.

'Leave that *book*, Ellie. You have to retreat.'

'Just a minute.'

'If you don't retreat I'll massacre you.'

'Oh, all right, but wait a bit.'

'You can't wait a bit if there's a war.'

'I'm reading something lovely.'

'Right. You'll be massacred. I'm coming. Over the top.'

She had always put down the book, but open and ready to go back to it, and sat dutifully down beside the soldiers. Charles had begun to talk in a clipped and military voice. A sweep of his arm had flattened multitudes.

'Surrender!'

'I always have to. All right. I do.'

'You're not much fun, Ellie. You put up no fight at all. I'm sick of you.'

'Play with Binkie then.'

'She says it's silly.'

'You mean she doesn't like losing.'

'She doesn't lose. She doesn't like the way I play. She hates me.'

'Well, you don't want me to hate you.'

'No. But I want you to fight.'

'I hate fighting. I'm reading.'

'Reading!'

'We're different, Charles.'

'We're not different. We' re *not* different. We've always been the same.'

'Yes. I know.'

The sun had shone in on the fallen troops and the Afghan carpet. The carpet had glowed like dark raspberries.

'You don't like fighting either really,' she'd said.

'Well, I won't ever have to.'

'Why?'

'This war will end all wars. It'll be over by Christmas. They say it all the time. There'll be great hurrahs at Christmas. Mama says we'll have the biggest tree to celebrate. The War won't last three months. When I get back from school.'

'When do you go?'

'September.'

'It's soon?'

'Two weeks.'

'Will you write?'

'Of course.'

'A lot?'

'Of course.'

She walked to pick up the book from the window seat and saw a servant putting tea-things on the terrace and people sitting there in careful attitudes. Mrs Frayling, statuesque herself, touched a carved boy eating grapes and twirled around a little silk parasol. She looked more old-fashioned than the rest but more beautiful. A man-servant came out with a massive silver tray. 'A tea-party first class,' she said to Charles. 'You'll have to go.'

'No. We'll be in the nursery with poor old dozy Pannell.'

'At a guess,' she said, 'at a *guess*, and the numbers of cups, you'll be wanted on the terrace.'

'How do you know?'

'There are unclish men with monocles and bored women with skirts too tight and floppety hats and nothing to say. It's being a terrible tea-party. Your mother is looking like Sainte Marie Madeleine peinte et dorée Souabe. Very ennuiée. She needs help.'

'What an awful lot you do know, Ellie.'

'Your mother taught me.'

'You like her, don 't you?'

She said, very surprised, 'Of course.'

'I don't,' he said. A flurry of starch and long ribbons ran in and said that Charles was to go to tea. 'On the terrace,' the maid added.

'C'mon,' he said.

'Not Ellie,' said the maid. 'Where's Miss Binkie? She's to go.'

'I'm not going without Ellie.'

'It's all right. I'm going home.'

'Say I'm not coming out without Ellie.'

'I'll do no such thing,' said the maid.

'Ellie and I are one person,' said Charles. The maid smiled and patted his brown hair. Ellie slid off the window seat and stepped through the soldiers: 'Keep my place,' she called, 'in the book,' and went off down the front stairs for once, since everyone was outside at the back of the house. She let herself out through the front door where a chauffeur of one of the guests leaned on a shining open car glittering with brasses like a coach. He jumped and looked guilty and ground out a cigarette under his heel when the door opened, then seeing only Ellie turned sulkily away and lit another. She passed him by and went down past the lodge, the drive and down the lane and through the village. It was half-day closing and her father's day off. Her father watered chrysanthemums. Her mother was cutting out a dress on the sitting room floor, her mouth spiked with pins. The dress was what Charles would have called headache pink and she mumbled through the pins that Ellie hadn't been expected back for tea. The house smelled of frying. The windows were shut.

It was the end that day, Elinor thought now, putting Terence into his crib. Even though I went back again, that day was the end. I was fourteen. Now I'm thirty-six. Yet it has never changed for me.

The deep silence from the rest of number three Seaview Villas seemed to suggest that there was a formidable audience somewhere in the house considering Ellie. In fact all grew so still that she became afraid and walked out on to the landing. Her husband, her daughter and Lydia were all downstairs in the tiny house, yet there was not a sound. Even the baby slept. Pressing about her alertly were a dozen sad ghosts.

Mother and Father knew, she thought. They knew how I loved being at the Hall but they never asked about it. I suppose they thought it was charity. It was a different age. It was mediaeval. The War was supposed to change it all. I wonder if it was the first real revolution. All wars are meant to change it all.

What a very odd thing to have thought, she said to the staircase wall and walked back into her bedroom. That's what the book was—the one I was reading that day. It was *War and Peace* and I've just remembered. I never did finish it. But it's what it was about—war not changing anything.

There was a long hollow crumpling noise from far away across the sand dunes which might have been a storm if it had not been such a balmy evening. 'Nothing changes anything,' she said.

Not that Charles ever found out. He never did fight in a war in the end. He was eighteen when it was over and he went up to Cambridge. Binkie was there already and me in the post office helping Mother.

Yet I was on the Czar's side and they were Socialists. 'Not Bolsheviks of course,' Binkie used to say. I'd always have been on the aristocrats' side because of their hair. I don't think I *could* have been a Roundhead. I can't bear their house now. Dene Close. Awful. Self-conscious. 'I'm just the same as you.' Plain man. Fabian stuff. I should never have gone there.

I should never have written the note when the doctor said I should see old friends again. I should never have gone. Especially with Margaret.

But, oh my, how she dealt with them.

She dealt with them. Suddenly Ellie was flooded with tremendous love for Margaret.

The full wonder of Margaret—so good and true and untroubling—brought tears into Ellie's eyes. She has a better brain than all of them, she thought. And she sees straight and clear. She's strong as a lion. The best thing in my life. The best thing in the world.

Margaret will trample his whole army down, thought Ellie. She'll rout him. She'll annihilate him. She's proud and good and strong. She's above the lot of them. He's a poor weed teaching at a council school—that's what's become of him—with his spinster sister keeping house. Margaret will show them! She'll end better than that. They'll see. She's the child his mother should have had, poor feeble Charles.

But I love him so, she thought looking out of the window out to sea. It hasn't changed.

Far across the pale light shiny water and the luminous sands she thought she saw Margaret picking her way out along the rocks to Eastkirk; then realised that this would be impossible.

But it's time she came in wherever she is, thought Ellie.

There was another queer flapping rolling uneasy noise like guns far away. Surely not thunder? 'It's getting late,' Ellie thought, 'and she's hardly over the mumps.'

# 14.

As Margaret followed her mother up to her bedroom, Binkie in Dene Close was making ready to go to Confession, for Elinor was a long way out of date talking about Fabians.

Binkie had cleared the tea-things and pegged the tea-cloth out to dry, washed her face and hands and changed her blouse for another of identical pattern but in which she had not rolled on the floor. 'I'll be an hour,' she called.

'Good heavens!' Charles called back. He was less close to Father Carter.

'Because,' said Binkie, 'I'm doing the flowers, too.'

'Do you do the flowers before or after?'

'It depends on the queue.'

'You can't do the flowers while you're *in* the queue.'

'Yes I can,' said Binkie, not adding that her confessor had vaguely suggested the unorthodoxy of this procedure, too. Binkie's flower-arranging in church involved a considerable banging of doors, vase-swilling in the vestry and tramping about flourishing branches. The confessional box backed on to the vestry and her vigorous feet.

'Doesn't it put people off?' asked Charles.

'Not at all. You take it too seriously, Charles. There's no need to be self-conscious about confession. It's a perfectly straightforward sacrament. Nothing to get het up about. Don't be such a Protestant.'

'I'm not. You don't have to be a Protestant to want to have

a chance to concentrate now and then. I thought you were supposed to be quiet beforehand. Before you started the long lament.'

'I'm sure *I* don't lament,' said Binkie, 'and I'm sure I have never in my life prevented anyone from being quiet.' She crashed across the hall and picked up a pair of massive secateurs which she dropped. 'One doesn't have to be so quiet, it seems to me. Look at the Catholics. They still have a lot to teach us, mistaken though they are about the Pope. Look at the churches of Italy.'

'I've never seen anyone like you, Binks, in the churches of Italy.'

'Well, of course not. We do not *fear* our priests.'

'I rather fear Father Carter. Or fear for him. He has a look of a man rushing towards a precipice.'

'Nonsense.'

'You are the pure Anglo-Catholic type, Binks.'

'I make no claims.'

'A washer-out of incense boats!'

'The acolytes do that. All that I am saying is that it is affected to try to be too quiet in church. One should be open and natural. In Africa all the little black babies run about the aisles.'

'You'd not catch Father Carter there.'

'Religion should be open. Out in the open.'

'Maybe you should be out on the sands with Ellie's husband.'

The slam of the sun-ray door reassured him that he had upset her and he felt affectionate towards her again. 'Old Binkie,' he thought, 'who'd have thought it. An Upper Second in Economics. Who'd have thought she'd have gone overboard for God. Or for Father Carter?'

But, too intricate a man to allow himself the common explanation, he dismissed this vulgarity at once and tried to think of

Binkie's confrontations with her Maker. He tried to think for example of the impossible image of her at confession. What in the world did she confess? A stalwart campaigner for her own humility and ordinariness, her meticulous life, her steady kindness—unsmiling, steady kindness certainly, but then—you don't know that you're unsmiling. You shouldn't be blamed for it. Unsmilingness is not necessarily blameworthy.

Sins of ignorance? Did Binkie ask forgiveness for sins of ignorance? Had she addled that much?

Charles walked about the house in the lovely hour of late summer afternoon. He had nothing in the world to do. It was still the school holidays—not one book to mark. The dry hot little garden was impeccable, the marble boy opening his mouth to the ever-uneaten grapes, the house shone—not a teacup left to put away. His study was full of beautifully-kept books and as neat as an office. Not a bill on his desk to deal with, not a letter to answer. He sat down at the desk and thought vaguely of the thesis he had kept going through the years on European Battlefields. The notes for it in six pale yellow folders lay on the farthest shelf from him across the room. This was the front of the house, away from the evening sun, but the light still beat in on the distempered walls, the ultra-modern tubular furniture. The only important colour in the room was the ruby red of the Afghan rug he had brought from home when the loonies had moved in. Binkie had said, 'I'll take nothing. I want nothing. Let her be.' (Later she had taken the marble boy.) But Charles had wanted to take very much—all the pictures, just one of the small landscapes would have been comfort. But the battle had been very terrible and he had made his choice. 'We'll have *nothing*,' Binkie cried. 'How could you want anything, after what she's done? She can give them the lot. I'm surprised you can think of *anything* you want now she's taken Ellie from you.'

'Taken Ellie?'

'Stopped you having Ellie.'

'Stopped me?' He had developed a slow, sweet almost tender way of speaking since his mother had vetoed Elinor, like a very old man, an old, old emperor above material things, too old for campaigning. At his school where he taught English literature he was considered now as rather a joke, with his pipe and his stately ways and his old-world accent—and still under forty. They had increased and over the years he had developed by now an air of regal distance from ordinary questions of the day, and so successfully, he thought, that now that I am back here near home there is no one in the world who dares ask me a personal question.

'Did you never think of getting married, Frayling?'

'Did you never feel like a bit of fun then, Charles?'

Nobody to say this.

He was witty and charming and sweet-tempered and good-looking and sexless—there was certainly no question even of homosexuality about him. That would have shown up in the school at once. Both the trench-survivors and the others who like himself had missed the terror were agreed upon it. 'He's a scholar,' it was at length decided, 'a real scholar. He writes, you know—law books and so forth, I believe. He'd meant to be a doctor, didn't you know? No—he was in the war—shell-shocked. You can always tell. No. He was too young, believe it or not. Tubercular? There's money, you know—there's still money. Very well-to-do. Old family. He was never expected to do much—they didn't have to in those days. County family.'

'They've got an air to them, him and that sister, now even.'

'The confidence of the very rich,' thought Father Carter watching Binkie shaking out albs and cottas and calling rather loudly to the organist. 'There are still some pictures somewhere.' The priest preparing for confessional considered a new reredos and thought—and then felt shamed—about the need for better guttering.

Yet life was frugal really at Dene Close. Except for the very occasional tea-party it was margarine rather than butter and their own rather leathery lettuce. Sunday lunch pudding was always a plain jam roll covered in packet custard and supper was hard-boiled egg with potted anchovy paste. The Fraylings drank no more alcohol than the Saints and seldom took a holiday.

Charles earned not quite five hundred a year and a few pounds from private tuition in the evenings and of this gave Binkie most for the housekeeping. She managed spendidly, went to bed early, read the works of George Macdonald and gave the rest of her life to her brother except for alternate Thursday afternoons when she visited her mother, returning less sure after each visit whether there was any point in carrying on with them. The great divide over Ellie Marsh had not been closed even by Mrs Frayling's hideous imprisonment so many years later.

Charles never visited her. He had not been to the Hall since he left it twelve years ago with only the Afghan rug slung into the back of the Austin motor car which he could not now afford. Even as he had slung the rug into the car he had felt her eyes on him from the windows, unrepentant and unrelenting. Not knowing he knew she was there, the ruminative face, the fine probing nose. He had seen her think—'How curious—a rug!'

'Why that?' even Binkie had said. Things were said between them for a while that would now be quite impossible.

'I'm not leaving it for the bloody mad.' It had been such an uncharacteristic remark that they had both remembered it and 'bloody mad' were the words he associated with the rug ever after when he looked down at it in the box of a room in Dene Close which they called The Study and in which he studied nothing.

He stared at the rug now, thinking that such an empty beautiful afternoon was perfect for a return to the European

Battlefields, and traced the pattern on it with his toe thinking of every one of its thousands of knots being tied separately by brown Afghan hands. In the queer silence that sometimes falls in rooms where there are a lot of books on still afternoons he thought, I am a portrait. This room and I are a portrait. He felt benign, gentle and good—even rather beautiful. It is enough, he thought, that I exist. There is no need any more—the pale yellow folders were delicate and distant in the yellower light. They looked peaceful enough and it was summer-time. Winter nights are for scholarship. There is no need any more for me to do a thing. He imagined the pleasure his tall aesthetic figure must give to passers-by—a touch of style, of imperturbability. He rearranged his gently sloping shoulders a little and ran a hand across his soft hair and picked up his pipe. He leaned back.

Directly below him the front-door bell began to ring, shrill as a drill as though it would never stop.

# 15.

'Teach me the disregard of every creature so that the Creator may be found,' Binkie prayed, jabbing big yellow daisies in an altar vase. She stood back and looked at them. The yellow howled at the Dean Inge blue and blood-red of the altar frontal and the healthy complexions of the twelve apostles who huddled in groups to either side of it in robes as brilliant. The niches for the servers and the carpets and hassocks for the acolytes were in the same jolly hues. Binkie had embroidered some of them herself. The jar she had chosen for the flowers was the boldest brass and there was a huge purple banner above her head where a pelican pulled feathers out of itself for its young above several large Greek declarations in gold and silver thread. 'Very nice,' she thought. 'Nice and bright.' A long hard-stemmed daisy began slowly to fall out of the pot. It collapsed to the ground as if it had fainted.

'Lord bring me self-renunciation,' prayed Binkie. 'Self-denial and the renouncing of every evil appetite. I need some bits of green.'

She went out through the vestry door, then out of the back door of the church leaving both doors open and snapped a few branches of yellow privet which had been planted there to mask the horrors round the grave tap—greasy vases and heaps of dead flowers. She ran the tap and let water drum into a can. With haphazard extra privet held before her in a bush and the extra water held before that and out of her range of vision she strode back into the chancel. 'Let me attain to entire resignation of myself and obtain freedom of heart. Give me good government of things external and not fretful of matters of business.' Missing her step as she passed the back of the confession box she cannoned into it and spilled water, dropped the can and gave a loud cry. Bezeer-Iremonger, who was finishing his confession round the other side, fell back in disorder and Father Carter within closed his eyes and paused for a moment before continuing absolution.

'Oh Lor!' called Binkie. She gathered herself up and shouted, sorry, trying to brush water off her skirt. 'Sorry! (Let me put my trust in God and I must get the dustpan and brush for the glass, when the arrows of the world assail us.)'

The privet looked very messy on the chancel steps and the water had left dark stains. The rest of the flowers had fallen out and lay around as if they had been flung by some explosion. As Mr Bezeer-Iremonger shuffled off there was nobody left but their scattered corpses and herself and Father Carter waiting in the box, and it was time for her to go to him and kneel down.

But the privet looked dreadful and how could she leave glass all over the place? How hot, how hot it was. Perhaps after all she would not make her confession today. She would discipline herself by being very patient and steady in gathering up the flowers instead. All grievous things—Father Carter drew back his little curtain and coughed summoningly—are to be endured for the sake of eternal life.

He coughed again. Perhaps she had better go. Leaning to the flowers was making her flush. If the glass cut someone . . . It was odd how she gave such an impression of capability, when really . . . Just look at the glass! I am so indecisive, she thought. So indecisive. Yet my shape is the shape of a stalwart woman who can proceed steadily towards goals.

She knelt.

In the name of the Father and Son and Holy Ghost, O

Lord, I have sinned . . . Behind the curtain Father Carter leant his attentive ear as the formal words flowed on.

And nobody knows, she thought, what it costs to live the life I live. The ordered life. All the tins, in the cupboards, with all the different coloured tops. Bedroom day Thursday, drawing room day Friday, baking day Wednesday, Charles's shirts all perfectly ironed by Tuesday after being perfectly washed on Monday. The milk-money ready in the hall, exact to the halfpenny every Saturday and the side door unlocked each week on dustbin day at precisely five minutes to seven. Every Sunday after lunch the cleaning out of the inside of the gas oven to catch the grease still hot. All grievous things are to be endured for the sake of eternal life.

They are not, though.

She did not endure. She did not readily endure the tyranny of the laundry list, the milk man, the grocery order for the sake of eternal life. She endured it because it was the lesser endurance. It kept her so busy that she need not think. If she stopped for a second to think, then the game would be up. Chaos would take charge. The sea would rush in and give up its dead. If she missed the three-fifteen for instance every other Thursday to Eastkirk to visit Mother, then she would find that time empty and reason might take over. Real issues might be broached then—such as why are you visiting her anyway? What are you doing? Where are you going? Since you hate her and have always hated her even before she emasculated Charles, why do you go at all? Since you despise Charles for having ever listened to her and for not marrying Ellie Marsh, why do you even iron his shirts? And since you despise Ellie Marsh for being so limp and simple, and since you are in your heart pleased that he didn't marry her and she is therefore nothing deeply to do with you, why do you see her again? Invite her to tea again after ten years? Fuss over the child?

Why do you care whether or not her child likes you? Why are you so ashamed that her child saw you looking a guy, sprawled on the floor, spilling cakes?

'I hate my mother,' she suddenly announced to the priest.

There was a sort of shuffle and glint from behind the grille and a clearing of the throat.

'He thinks I've gone wonky,' she thought. 'Thinks I'm a bit funny.'

'Hate, loathe and detest her,' she said again, loudly. (Oh, if thou hadst seen the everlasting crowns of the saints in heaven and with how great glory they now rejoice . . . )

'I despise my mother, and my brother and I hate my life with him. There is nobody I do not hate or despise. Nobody on earth ( . . . who once were esteemed in the world as contemptible. Neither wouldst thou long for this life's pleasant days . . . ).'

'My child . . . ' (behind the grille.) 'You are repenting of this?'

'No.'

'I see. Then . . . '

'I am not repenting. I am telling you that I am filled with hate and that I am not repenting.'

(Her age.) 'My child, let me . . . '

He came out of the box and helped her up and walked her to the front pew. The church was quite empty.

'This is a shock,' he said. 'It's a shock, Binkie . . . '

'I've had a blow,' she said and began to scream a little. '"I've had a blow, Jane".'

(Right off it. Round the twist.) 'Binkie, I had no idea . . . '

'I was at Girton,' she wept.

'Yes—yes, I know.'

'It was the best time of my life. When Charles came up—the year after me, he took me about. May Balls . . . '

'I'm sure . . . ' Father Carter looked about him. The twelve apostles looked unflinchingly back. 'I'm sure it must be dull. Dull for you now. Here. It is a very great waste . . . '

Through her tears the words of Thomas a Kempis went straying on. 'Oh if these things had a sweet savour and pierced to the bottom of thy heart how couldst thou dare so much as once to complain?' Then she thought that he had said something about her waist.

He had said she was fat.

'I was thin. I was thin as could be,' she wept, looking into his face. 'At Cambridge. If you'd known me then . . . '

(Oh Lord!)

'I got a good Upper Second. I had several chances to marry. But I couldn't get away, you see. *Do* you see? Do you know what it's like with a woman like my mother in the background? She ruins everything. Ruins. Ruins. Destroys. She sneers and watches. Even now she sneers and watches. Laughed at Charles wanting to marry Ellie. Laughed at me from the beginning because I couldn't play the piano—didn't like her beastly pictures or want to read her ghastly books. She hated us so much one summer she used to run off out of the house and walk about on the beach. Just to get away from us. She used to burst into tears at breakfast. She *killed* my father—he just sat wondering why he was hated. Then at Cambridge she laughed at Charles and me for being Socialists. She gave the house to charity just to watch what we'd do about it. Disinherited us, she said, "Now see how you like equality." She is a vile woman. She has ruined my life.'

'I believe,' said the priest, 'that she is very sick . . . '

'And Charles's.'

'Binkie—Miss Frayling—she is dying.'

Red as a bull Binkie blew her nose and roared, 'So are we all.'

They sat silently together and Father Carter took off his stole and held it between his hands fingering the silk threads in it, threads worked by another Binkie in the parish before—a loving present when he left. 'Another of them. Another—' he thought. 'So many. It was the War. Not enough men left.' Binkie covered her splendid face up in a handkerchief and the unending summer sun beat on through the bright windows.

She thought, 'Oh, if these things had a sweet savour for thee and pierced to the bottom of thy heart, how couldst thou dare so much as once to complain? Are not all painful labours to be endured . . . ?'

'I've left the privet.'

'Privet?'

'All over the chancel. And broken glass.'

'I'll see to it.' He held her hand.

Then he helped her from the church and they trailed together over the graveyard to the vicarage wicket gate (Bezeer-Iremonger was studying a headstone in the graveyard with interest) where he held it open for her and put across her shoulder a comforting arm and Bezeer-Iremonger bent to the headstone with greater attention. 'But it's not true,' she cried across the graves loudly, making him jump.

'It's not true. I don't hate *everybody*.'

'Of course not.'

'I don't hate you, Father. And I do really love children.' She began to weep again.

He took her over the vicarage lawn in the bright calm evening. The pink houses in streets and crescents lay peaceful in the hot light, basking all around. Along the Front people trudged up sandy from the beach, dragging spades and the hands of children. A few solid old buildings and the lifeboat house stood out, reminding anyone who cared to be reminded that the place had once been a fishing village. Fishing boats pulled up on the promenade still pointed their prows upwards to the heavy blue of the sky. A place at peace, the War long past, the stench of the trenches gone, thought Father Carter.

And here are the survivors—strong and well and bitterly unhappy. With nothing to do. Whatever has Christianity to offer this one? What is there to be done for her, poor thing. Intelligent—and trying her best. He settled her on the vicarage sofa.

'The C of E breeds them,' he thought, offering her a very small sherry. 'God knows what's to be done.'

## 16.

On the doorstep Ellie stood. She said, 'I've left him.' Charles held the door, still dazed from the emptiness of the afternoon. Behind him the dazzling light in the clean little house, nothing displaced, nothing brewing, simmering or boiling; supper set and complete on the trolley covered by a cloth, the ham and salad hygienically out of sight in the larder. Here in front of him on the step was the woman he had nearly married over twelve years ago, in an untidy blouse, hair blown about and a red face and tears running diagonally from her eyes to the base of each ear. He said vacantly, 'I was in my study.'

'I've left him!'

'Oh . . . ' He looked round thinking to see an empty pram about somewhere. 'The poor child!'

'I've left my husband. Kenneth. Let me in.'

'My dear Ellie . . . '

'Where's Binks . . . ? Oh, Charles . . . ! I must lie down.'

He wavered about the hall and looked in the sitting room. Upright chintzes and pouffes. 'I'm afraid there isn't anywhere exactly . . . very . . .

'We—I—we haven't got a spare bed.' He leapt after her. 'Just the two bedrooms. The other is my study. You'll have to—er—lie—on Binkie's.'

Opening Binkie's door, however, her bed was seen to be covered and stacked with great neat heaps of clothing, books and trays of jam awaiting collection.

'Oh, Lord, the bazaar! Oh, Ellie—there's a church bazaar. Next Saturday . . . '

'For goodness sake, Charles!' Ellie flew past him and burst into the next-door bedroom—his own—and flung herself headlong on his bed. 'Am I here for bazaars?' She began to weep noisily into the folk-weave bedcover.

Her outline was large and loose and soft and she sank down, denting the bed, and looked, in spite of the desperate way she rubbed her face about in the pillow, very much settled there.

'Ellie,' he said standing near. The sobs increased and he touched her shoulder. 'I'll get some brandy.'

'We never drink it. It isn't permitted.'

'Are you at boarding school?'

'Yes.' She sobbed harder. 'Yes, yes, yes. Or a mad house. I don't know. Oh, Charles!'

'But you've been married to him twelve years.'

'Yes.'

'And had two children.'

'Yes.'

'But you go . . . go in for it all, don't you? You must have believed in it—all the sin and so forth. Somewhere in you you must have believed in it? It can't have been just because of . . . '

She sobbed. 'Of what?' she said at last.

'Well—well—because of me.'

'How dare you. How *dare* you! What did you think you meant to me? Conceit—utter, utter conceit. The whole family the same . . . '

'I'm sorry, Ellie. I just thought—all that sin . . . I couldn't see you thinking . . . It was out of character, Ellie.'

'I don't know. How should I know?'

'I'll get the brandy.'

He brought two huge brandies and she sat up and drank

hers in one swallow. He took the glass from her and walked across the room with his own to the window. Looking out over the municipal park with its prominent litter bins and carefully spaced dahlias he thought, 'Brandy in the bedroom. With Ellie. In the afternoon.'

'Did you mind meeting me again, Ellie? The other day?'

'I wouldn't have invited myself to tea if I had.'

'You looked so very . . . cool.' He turned round to the flushed plump creature in this bed. At fourteen it had floated like a wisp on his windowsill, so slight and fragile that she might perhaps only be some sort of trick of the light, or a ghost in the old house, her huge soft eyes turning to him but seeing things elsewhere in a less physical world. Ellie the dustman's ethereal daughter. Now however he saw with consternation that she was taking off her clothes.

'Ellie! Binkie will be back in a minute!'

'Binkie!' She wrenched off her blouse and dropped it on the floor.

'She's at confession.'

'Confession!'

'She doesn't take very long usually. She'll be back any minute. She never takes long, even when she's doing the flowers.'

'Flowers!' Ellie had turned back the bedcover and was taking off her stockings. 'Whatever's Bink to do with flowers? They'd drop dead soon as look at her.'

'You've become very abrasive,' he said with interest—but not with commendation. Ellie had been—and it had been her charm—unswervingly adoring of the Fraylings.

'And *confession*! I ask you. How typical.'

'You are more analytical than I remember.'

She began to laugh helplessly. 'Good Lord—Good Lord! What a thing to say. More analyt . . . I wonder just what you do remember?'

'A peaceful person,' he said, 'gentle. Loving. You know what I remember, Ellie.'

'Ha!' She was now undoing an enormous camisole.

'Ellie . . . look. Could you stop? I think you're not very well.'

'Quite right.'

'What *happened*?'

'I've had a revelation.' She got herself out of her skirt. 'If I were Margaret I would quote you chapter and verse, but at least I missed the Sunday School so I'm not trained to that. I only had your mother and Miss Pannell.' She dragged up his sheets, slid deep down into his bed and turned her face to the wall. 'I've been in a mad house, Charles. A mad house. I didn't know it till this afternoon when I . . . walked past an open door. If you knew—if you and Bink knew. If you had ever known what passion is all about. What madness is all about. It would be very good for you to know—the pair of you. You never will. Madness will never get near you. Leave me alone. I must have some sleep.'

'We do know,' he said, 'about mad people. People who live in mad houses seldom . . . throw stones.'

After a while during which she looked at the wall and he turned and stared out of the window again, she said, 'I'm sorry,' and began once more to cry.

Charles watched a car draw up at the gate. Out of it stepped Father Carter who opened a door for Binkie who emerged heavily, followed by the shambling figure of Bezeer-Iremonger, and the trio moved up the path. Charles said, 'Hell. Oh, Hell. Whatever next!'

'What?' she sobbed.

'Look, Ellie—could you stop crying? Er . . . darling! Binkie's here.'

'Well, I don't care. I don't want to talk to her now.'

'She's got a priest with her.'

'Well, maybe that'll be a good thing.'

'Ellie—whatever's the matter with you? I've never known you like this in your life. It may be over twelve years, but . . . you're histrionic. A child would be more rational. Bezeer-Iremonger is with the priest.'

'Christ!' she said, sitting up and staring.

There was a booming and clattering in the hall below. 'No—Bezeer-Iremonger,' he said, and steadily they held the look between them. Elinor said, 'I am not laughing,' and began to. 'Charles!' cried Binkie, thumping up the stairs.

'Shut me in. Quick!' said Ellie. 'Go away.'

'I love you,' he said.

'Shut me in. I love you. Go away.'

He thought, she has authority—she's as certain of herself as Binkie. More so. She is changed. And there is something else—something Binkie hasn't got—yet something familiar. A simplicity he had met recently and loved, though not in her. Yet it was Ellie—it was the Ellie he had always known with something much better as well. She had confidence. It had been the lack of confidence in her that had troubled him. She had been a heavy, introverted child, a heavy-going girl-friend, easily forgotten behind the grille of the village post office when he had gone to Cambridge. And there had been the inexcusable touch of deference. Of . . . well, almost obsequiousness behind her shyness and self-conscious skipping walk. 'Shut the door and go away,' she cried now, half-naked, pulling his sheets over her head and turning her face to the wall. Around his bed her clothes were scattered in a preposterous heap.

'Coming!' he cried out to his sister, and nearly cannoned into her on the landing.

'Father Carter has kindly said,' announced Binkie, 'that he will take the things to the bazaar. We picked up Mr Bezeer outside the vicarage and he says he'll help. It's a good chance. They are all on my bed.'

Bezeer-Iremonger was roaming up the stairs and making for

Charles's door. 'No—this way, Mr Beezer. Charles—go down and talk to Father Carter.'

'Er—no. I'll help. You go down. He might like a brandy.'

'A brandy!' Binkie's big face grew huge. 'At *this* time in the evening?'

'Perhaps Mr Bezeer would like a brandy?' Bezeer-Iremonger who had been looking hard at Charles's door brightened up. Charles said. 'Though you don't drink, Mr Bezeer, do you? Aren't you a Primitive?'

'Nonsense,' shouted Binkie heartily. 'Mr B is nothing of the sort, I've just followed on from him at confession. Give him the jam to carry. You take the books. Perhaps Father C might follow and kindly take a few clothes? Then perhaps we could all have another sherry.'

'Another . . . ?'

'Well, we had some at the Vicarage.'

'I see,' said Charles surprised.

'I didn't,' said Bezeer-Iremonger, 'and I haven't got long.'

'Oh dear,' said Charles.

'You two go ahead.'

The three trooped down the stairs with the armfuls of lumber. 'Might I help?' asked Father Carter in the hall.

'Yes. There's a lot more,' Binkie said, 'just on my bed.'

'Hold on—I'll show you,' Charles shouted. He began to run with the jam at full speed to the car. 'Hold on,' and made it back in time to find Father Carter safely approaching the right bedroom. 'Oh, sorry,' he said slowing down, 'just thought you might get the wrong room.'

'The door was open,' said the priest.

'Just thought you might have got to my study by mistake. Gathered up the wrong stuff.'

'I don't suppose you keep heaps of clothes in your study,' Father Carter said politely. 'By the way, Frayling, I wonder if I could have a word with you some time?'

'I'm afraid . . . I'm afraid . . . ' Charles looked wildly around, 'I can't take anything on just at present. A book nearing completion . . . er . . . writing up an old thesis.'

'No, no. Nothing to do with the parish. I know you are not . . . convinced. It is about your sister. She is in some difficulty. A spiritual difficulty.'

'Hello there?' called Binkie's restored and rolling voice from below. 'Can you manage?'

'Yes, yes,' said Charles.

'She's . . . I'm afraid, quite deeply disturbed.'

'Charles!' roared Binkie. 'Whatever are you doing? The jam is sliding all over the seat. Ridiculous place. You practically threw it.'

'Hatred,' said the priest, 'is so very close to love.' There was a scuffly noise behind him from the closed door and Charles shouted loudly, 'It'll be all right. You'll just have to hold the tray when you go round the corners.'

'As,' said Father Carter, 'sanity is so close to madness. Is that a dog?'

'We haven't got a dog. It must be the wind.'

'Wind—ah,' said Carter mopping his head in the boiling, airless house. 'As of course we all know. I often think, Frayling, someone who *consciously*, *fiercely* strives after sanity, after an image of sanity—a person with perhaps not quite enough to do, someone with a real sense of being an example to the rest of us—such a person is at terrible risk.'

'I'm sending up Bezeer,' called Binkie threateningly.

'No. No. We're on our way.' Charles tried to urge Carter down the stairs ahead of him. 'Can you see your way?' Carter feeling for the top step hidden by the tall pile of white elephants swung a foot about in mid-air for a while and there was another vibration from behind Charles's door. Carter turned to it. 'Just as someone who is immensely loving,' he said, 'I always feel is capable of equal hatred—don't you? And we all need *objects* of love—except of course the saints. That does sound like a dog?'

'We haven't got one.'

'Ah.'

'Shall we go down?' Charles gave the priest a shove, for Bezeer-Iremonger was coming up. They crossed with him on the stairs. At the car, alone with Carter for a moment again, they stacked things and steadied the jam. 'Of course she's at a difficult age. She needs a lot of *love*,' Carter murmured.

'Of course. Precisely,' said Charles and saw with relief that Binkie, unloved, was sailing down the path to join them followed by Bezeer-Iremonger, who had the last few bits and pieces of clothing trailing about him. 'A drink?' he urged half-heartedly. Bezeer-Iremonger blinked with hope.

'No. No. We won't trouble you, Frayling. (She's had a sherry or two already.) Better get this stuff safely stowed. Bezeer will be responsible for the jam. Bezeer—get in,' and Bezeer got lugubriously in, one arm embracing the toppling jars, the other still clutching the last small heap of garments which Charles saw with a queer sudden dizziness. Binkie settled herself beside the driver, a stack of old books balanced on her knee up to and past eye-level.

'How unattractive these things always look until they are *displayed*,' said Carter. 'I never cease to wonder how we make money at these parish beanos.'

'Yes.'

'Remember what I said.' He shook hands meaningfully. 'Can we discuss this further? She is most *insecure*.' He turned his head away from Binkie's ears. 'Needs a family. Women need someone to command.'

'Father, we must be moving,' Binkie boomed, 'Mr Beezer is meant to be singing in five minutes on the sands.'

'But splendid woman, of course. *Vale*!' he added, lifting a thumb.

'*Non mecum*,' said Charles, getting out a handkerchief and mopping hands and face. '*Gratias*.'

He staggered back to the house thinking what a tatty old mystery Bezeer was.

But then maybe no more than anyone else.

Sanity, insanity, he thought. Love, hate. Sense, nonsense. And where shall wisdom be found?

Even the things Bezeer touched seemed to turn rubbishy, he thought, and wondered why the last armful of clothing had seemed so familiar. He couldn't remember. He couldn't connect. And this was the second time today that he couldn't connect.

The first had been when he had looked at Ellie's shining face, clear and young and courageous in his bed. And now, these clothes.

He locked the front door behind him and picking up the brandy bottle on the way, returned to his room.

On opening the door he remembered both things at once. For Ellie, wrapped up in the folk-weave, glared at him with the wide blue eyes of the child Margaret. It was Margaret I saw, he thought—Ellie is just one part of Margaret. The other thing he remembered as he looked at the floor.

'That awful old man,' said Ellie, above the counterpane, 'came in and took away my clothes.'

# 17.

A troop of dogs was rushing around the sands, four chasing one, and all very excited with their tongues hanging out. Margaret watched them tearing about. There was a great big black one with matted sandy hair, a hot red one with hot red eyes and a tail in a curl, and a white midget with legs like trotters. The dog they chased was a nondescript-looking, slightly mangy Airedale and it seemed distressed. As Margaret watched, the big black dog leapt on its back and began to push it vigorously along in jerks. She did not feel that she dare rescue it herself—the black dog seemed so fierce—but she couldn't think why nobody else tried. There were still quite a lot of people on the beach for the tide was far out.

Children were just beginning to be called in. Mothers were packing up beach–bags or finishing a last cigarette. Several men were there, too. But most people were not even watching the dogs and some had quite turned away. They wriggled about in strange attitudes beneath towels, getting out of their bathing clothes, feeling about modestly for underclothing. The other dogs—the ones who had not leapt on the Airedale's back—sat down in a semi-circle and watched and waited, panting. Margaret said to a small boy bashing a sandcastle with the flat of a spade, 'Look at the poor dog.' He looked and turned to his father and yelled, 'Dad!'

'Eh?' The man was lying on the sand with his heels and shoulders pressed into it and the rest of him heaved into an arc under a towel. He flung off a rag of bathing trunks with his foot and turned a tortured face to the dogs and went on squirming.

'The dogs,' cried the boy.

'Shurrup,' said the man.

'What are they doing?' Margaret asked. The man had now stood up and was tucking a long old shirt into flannel bags. His wife, picking up rugs, her cigarette dropping long ash, sniggered. 'Git on,' said the man. 'Nowt.'

The boy had already lost interest and gone back to the keep of his castle. 'It might get hurt,' said Margaret. Nobody said a word. Instead of words they all seemed to be breathing out something which Margaret felt disturbing and familiar and she turned away.

She walked on out towards the sea which was only a line in the distance beyond the rocks. Even the end of the pier was bare today, its poor thin chicken's legs stuck in big cement humps with rusty marks trickling over them. She walked on until she reached the place where the sand was hard with sahara ripples, and pressed her shoes into every ridge to spoil it. There were heaps of sand worms. Worm casts, her mother called them, but Margaret knew better. They were little bundles of live worms created from sand as God had created Adam out of spit and dust. They looked like chestnut purée.

Now there were pools as clear as glass and she waded through them until they got more frequent and deeper and were able to soak through her shoes and socks. The tops of her ankle socks were dark worm-chestnut brown, fawn purée. Fawn, worm-shaped and sopped. Sand collected inside them and it grew uncomfortable. The rocks began, long and black, ridged crocodiles, covered with barnacles. If you pounced quickly enough upon a barnacle you could just feel it move. Just the faintest looseness and then—clamp! Rock to rock. Dust to dust. How old are barnacles? How old do they grow? What becomes of dead barnacles? Where do old barnacles go to die? Rock of ages cleft for me. How tightly stuck to the rock was the barnacle? How tightly stuck had been the big black dog? Why had the woman sniggered?

Two white hands on Lydia's back. Lydia's wide tight back. White back beneath the big pink corset. White, tight hands over the hidden, ridged corset. White beneath.

And God said Thou shalt love one another. That is my Commandment.

And so why do I feel . . .

The pools were not pools now, they were lakes. She had walked a very long way. When she turned there were rocks and pools behind her and the huge beach shining like a steel sheet, then the pale line of the dry sandcastles with the crackling seaweed, the sweet-papers and the litter. Behind this again the promenade and the railings—though she was too far out now to see the railings. She could not even see Seaview Villas from here, only the small crinkled gables in a little low rick-rack line. She was way beyond the pier's end.

It was a grand square platform, the pier's end—she'd not seen it before from the sea—or where the sea should be. Its little box theatre was perched on the end of it. Nobody stood around the fishermen with the sea and the fish had all gone away. Though there was a gleam now about the foot of the pier—a luminous hazy look. And the humps of cement seemed to be smaller.

She turned and went on—sploshing down into a pool. When one pool was deep and reached up over her thighs she gave a gasp of delight, for she was very wet now. She stumbled and fell forward and saved herself on a rock, grazing her hand. She sat on a rock and looked at the hand, wishing that it had been hurt more badly.

Why?

And why was it not all right for white hands to be moving over a back? Why should not her father love Lydia?

Why did it make her feel sick? Like she felt sick when her mother crooned and moaned over the baby? She had felt sick when her mother cried over the brawn. She had felt a bit sick—a bit excited but a bit sick—watching all those dogs. I wish—she thought, and wondered what.

To talk, she thought. Someone to talk to.

She got up and walked still further out among the rocks and watched how the water had begun to move in over them not very far away in front of her, how it came in from two directions and sometimes fast. Faster all the time.

As she watched, it began to hit the rocks with slaps. It spilled over the rock she stood on. Over her shoulder too she could see that it was running behind her, with a determined, throaty noise, a rumble almost, then a splash and then a pause.

A white frill appeared along each rock about her feet and still further out it seemed to have got beyond the stage of frills. Each hard edge was backed by a definite lacy flounce, and there—goodness!—there was a frill of white at the top of a flounce. A spray, almost a fountain. The water curled and had become here and there bulging, ragged and awry—it had become almost waves. Behind her she saw to her surprise that the rocks she had hop-scotched over even a minute ago had quite disappeared and she was looking out over a wet, foamy muddle of shallow water. 'Better get back,' she thought, but felt tired suddenly.

All the soft chestnut serpents were disentangling beneath the water, all the barnacles whistling with relief, launching themselves from the dark anchorages, safe and swimming free, far from plucking claws. 'A hiding place is not a home,' said Mr Drinkwater. She thought longingly of the dry hot garden and the dry earth beneath his gigantic wellington boots. Of a distant time and place—of peace.

('Were you ever bored?'

'Never, never, never.')

Then she thought for some reason of the huge liquid eyes of the wooden woman.

'But where shall wisdom be found? And where is the place of understanding?' Job twenty-eight twelve. 'Not,' she thought, 'not there'—looking for the gables of Seaview Villas.

But the weather had changed and darkened and home was nowhere to be seen. She turned her face out to the incoming sea and splashed on.

## 18.

Charles thought, Lord, she's fat! How fat she is. Large and sleepy and fat. Beautiful though. She was always beautiful. It's over twelve years—I've scarcely thought of her. And she's in my bed.

And without her clothes.

There was always something silly about her. She was always losing things, dreaming about, large-eyed and adoring, rather bigger than he was which had begun to be slightly foolish very early on. Loving her was there of course, secure beneath the embarrassment and the uncertainty of how she would measure up.

He could not remember a time before he had loved Ellie. He had been a scrap of a child dominated by the elder sister, almost invisible beside the beauty of the tall mother and the distinguished father whom he seemed in no way to resemble. Ellie's adoration had been a joke but it gave a glow of life when his family were not about and made him expand and parade. As they grew and she changed to a painfully self-effacing girl who sat too quietly with a book, and he passed from hoops and scooters to a bike and lead soldiers, her love had been a background fact he recognised like the sun on the garden wall in summer or the great spread of the gold elms. Still and quiet and almost looking flimsily aged at ten years old she had loved him and he had the blessing of having someone it was quite safe to hurt.

Ellie's love had borne him along on the first terrible journey to his prep school and the holidays from this establishment had seen little change between them. At Rossall the horrors of his gruesome thinness and inability to play games had been endurable the first term because of Ellie's securely waiting at home for the glory of his return. He had not much memory of this when he came to think about it. He had spent holidays away with people and much less time at home. When he tried to see her in the years after prep school he couldn't—only some tea-party of his mother's which he knew had been in some way important—but, with the war and the house being made into a nursing home, Ellie must have not been about so much.

Then Cambridge had knocked the whole thing on the head. It was not just the distance, he thought now, holding Ellie heavy and limp and partly-camisoled in his cardiganed arms; it was the new friends flying his own colours to whom his home and the North and the past meant nothing, who did not even particularly want to come to stay, who knew nothing and did not particularly care to hear about the beautiful mother with her long, meaning looks and liquid dresses and distant smile. Ellie, like the elms and the lawn and the bright green drawing-room and the marble boy on the terrace, became stage properties from another play and his independence of her no more tinged with guilt than if she had been a figure in a painting.

His vacations had mostly been spent on reading parties—Greek of a morning, stout boots in the afternoon—hearty times.

Bloomsbury and its wreaths of roses in the meadows had been over, the Somme survivors had either crept into corners or made a lot of noise throwing each other into the river rather more often than was necessary or enjoyed. Undergraduates were old young men or babies like Charles, finding only if they were lucky that Cambridge could still assert itself as important, that May Week and madrigals and saxophone music and hot nights in punts could turn one weak with pleasure on the unchanged river.

But 1919 Cambridge had not been made for love. Ladies had of course been present but the sculpted brisk creatures with straw hats and then no hats and shorn hair did not stir Charles's desire. He had grown a soft moustache. Excitement had come from apses, fan vaulting, plainsong by candlelight, surplices shining against glossy black oak. Binkie had renounced even this for the gnash of the Leavisites and the garrulity of the healthy Mr Bernard Shaw while Charles had pursued buttered toast and crumpets, claret and conversation in Fellows' rooms—leisure and freedom and books. There had been tremulous Forsterian breakfasts—hot muffins. Petals had fallen outside the window, floating from an old tree against a breathtaking dark April sky.

Scarlet beadles for his graduation—an excitement about the streets, white fur hoods, processions, young men laughing, champagne for breakfast. The wide green of the Backs with King's Chapel afloat in them made him think at last of home and Ellie.

He wrote to his mother to tell her to bring Ellie to his graduation too and enclosed a note to be sent her at once. The note, brought down from the Hall to the post office where Ellie worked, made her blink like an owl behind the sweet bottles—the post office was diversified—and the note so longed for, now that it was here, filled her of course with terror and dismay.

Throughout the day she had looked at it. 'You'll come to my graduation, Ellie? Mother and B will contact with all arrangements. My day is Wednesday. Wear a hat, love Charles.'

She had liked it less and less.

By tea-time it had the appearance of a sop, and by suppertime it was an insult. 'I shall not go,' she decided and threw it on the fire.

The post office 'phone rang and she heard Binkie.

'But of course you must. He's sent special instructions.'

'But I can't leave work, Binkie.'

'Oh, nonsense. There's somebody else. I'll see to it. Mother will.' (For the village post office was still the Frayling Post Office, with the day's letters from the Hall gathered up from the silver tray.) 'After all these years! You can't let him down. And you've never seen Cambridge.'

'No. I can't go. It's . . . too long ago, Binkie,' and it was only Mrs Frayling's arrival in a pony and trap the next morning that changed her mind. The bell had jingled on the shop door and Ellie had looked up from behind the metal trellis and seen, beside the sweets and the big bulging metal plates nailed to the wall saying Oxo and Mazawattee Tea, Mrs Frayling carefully examining bars of white milk chocolate and peppermints. She turned slowly—she was dressed in tussore and a dolman. There was fine piping on the long skirt and her hat rustled with roses and ribbons above her serious face.

'My son expects you at Queen's,' she had said, buying a penny and a penny-halfpenny stamp. 'We shall call at eight o'clock on Tuesday. I can help you with the correct clothes.'

Had she not added the last words several people's lives would have been otherwise: Ellie would have pushed the two stamps across the counter, thanked Mrs Frayling for saying she would take her to Cambridge, refused the invitation firmly and not needed to see any of the family again. Mrs Frayling's brooding, almost pulsating anxiety would have been at an end, the roses in the hat would have ceased to vibrate—and many words not been spoken between her and her son. A house would have been conventionally inherited and a number of lunatics less delectably housed. 'I will help you if you wish with the correct clothes,' said Mrs Frayling, and a family was scattered and another made possible.

'Thank you, that will be unnecessary. I have clothes,' Ellie had replied and had been ready for the railway station on

Tuesday with hat, gloves, and travelling costume which had taken all her savings but been carefully calculated to appear nothing more than adequate and in no way pretty. She held a small suitcase borrowed from the vicar's daughter, her head high and her plump face for the first time in her life carrying an expression of coldness and distaste. Binkie, returning to Cambridge apparently stolidly for the first time since her own graduation a year before, read the works of Sidney Webb all the way to Peterborough. Mrs Frayling in their first class carriage with its silky pillows and buttoned backs leant to the landscape and let the drab Plain of York pass by, trying not to detest the chilly composure of the village post-mistress who was passing the journey engrossed in a small volume which looked pathetically like Shakespeare.

Of course all the nonsense had been years ago—a childhood friendship. Ellie was receiving no more than the same kindness held out to her as a little girl when they had let her, in a traditional old English way, share the Hall governess.

She was a wisp. A girl they had all been good to. But in spite of Charles, was it not being cruel? Should they have let her come at all with them? Stay in their hotel? Wouldn't it make the poor child have hopes? How she would cope with Cambridge one could hardly conceive. One must simply pray that Charles would be of some assistance.

And of course dear Charles had been splendid—jocular almost. At lunch at the University Arms he had teased Ellie like a brother. Resplendent in royal blue and white fur hood, he introduced her to others in the same disguise. 'Our little friend,' he had said, 'from the village.'

Ellie had sat still as a stone through the degree ceremony, dazed by the scarlet of the Vice-Chancellor, the hat-doffing, the quaint holding of fingers, the Latin chant, the kneeling and pressing together of hands. When it was Charles's turn—so tall and controlled, almost as tall and controlled as the Vice-

Chancellor although he had only got a Third—Ellie had sat very still indeed. Had thought, 'We are one person.'

How unimportant that at the tea-party afterwards he had seemed to ignore her, left her standing in a crowd of strangers as he hunted out the strawberries and cream—and how like him that he had found only tea enough for his mother and Binkie—for he had forgotten to get some for himself as well. And they were one person.

In the late afternoon in King's College Chapel heads had turned towards the mother in a toque of pale net and a muslin dress, leaning on a parasol of the same material (is it the Queen?), saying good-bye to Binkie who was going to look up old friends at Girton. Charles spotted some old family friends too across the nave who came up laughing and everyone had gathered into a group. Ellie had walked away then up into the chancel and stood a moment at the altar rail looking at the great East window. Blue and gold and red it shone in the dark. Christ shown to the people. Ecce Homo.

A man was standing looking at the picture intently but without much apparent pleasure and she saw it was Kenneth Marsh from home.

'You're from home!' she said and felt thoroughly delighted. 'We were at school. Don't you remember? I didn't know you were at Cambridge.'

She remembered a wormish withdrawn little boy who had been hard-working but nothing more and whose father had a funny religion.

'I thought you were Chapel,' she said and laughed. 'I mean chapel like the one in Turner Street, not this one. Did you get invited by someone? I did—I came to see Charles Frayling.'

He said, 'I was invited by Jack Nattress. He hadn't got anybody. He was in our class at elementary.'

'Jack Nattress in standard six?'

'Yes. He got a scholarship.'

The two of them turned round and looked down the church to the jolly crowd of Fraylings in the middle of the centre aisle. Rosalie with sun falling on her astounding hair under the toque was saying something amusing. The others—and Charles in particular—stood about looking proud to be seen with her. The group looked self-sufficient, complete, as perfectly balanced as the coloured window.

I don't belong, Ellie thought, I shall never belong there. I am unnecessary to them, even to Charles. I am brought here for my education and they will say in years to come, 'Do you remember Charles's graduation? Wasn't that a beautiful day? D'you remember we took little Ellie from the post office—didn't she love it? She was helplessly in love with Charles, poor child, but she really behaved very nicely indeed. She shared our governess, you know . . . '

'God bless you,' said Kenneth Marsh quaintly, shaking hands. He went off down the chancel, passed the Fraylings without a glance, and was out of sight. 'What an elderly little man,' she had thought. 'What a sober person.' But what she had really felt important were his friendliness and the comfort of meeting a familiar face on unfamiliar ground.

Charles thought now in bed at Dene Close of Ellie's tender face so many years ago as she stood, far off as India, on the chancel steps of King's Chapel. That was the moment, he thought, when I knew I'd ask her to marry me. After that terrible shrieking strawberry tea. In King's Chapel—with Mother holding forth to Cousin Dossie and ignoring Ellie like a servant—Ellie all alone up there and looking at the sights with the tourists.

I decided then. But not because I loved her—that was the mistake. It was because I panicked.

I hadn't known how little I cared about women until I left home. I had never touched a woman in my life, or thought very much about them. I was uneasy—not more—that I never seemed able to joke about women, or even see the jokes about women. I suppose I was a cold fish, but I didn't let it trouble me much.

I was romantic, I thought, not sensual! There was always the knowledge that Ellie loved me when I felt perhaps that something was a bit awry.

I didn't love Ellie though—I did know that. Not now.

And then the day I saw myself with Mother—all my life with Mother, laughing at her jokes, arming her along in a group of her admirers, driving her about, more often as the years passed and her arthritis or whatever it was got worse. I saw myself smooth and fattish and forty and people saying, 'Oh, Charles is so good to his mother.' Ellie—it was perfectly clear—was the inevitable, the only possibility; familiar as my own hands and feet, and ready and waiting. She was like an old pair of shoes to be put on.

'We are one person,' I used to say when we were children, and I asked her to marry me before breakfast next morning in the foyer of the University Arms Hotel, before the others came down.

We had all the luggage packed for the journey home. It stood about the foyer. It was a sweet blowy warm June morning.

She said yes at once, looking astonished at herself and holding tight to the back of a high chair and we went out and walked down to the river and along the Backs in the green morning—few people about yet but the sun hot. Roses tumbled in heaps over Queen's walls. Long trestle tables from the night before stood about in cloisters. Empty champagne bottles leaned up in niches and fountains and at tipsy angles in gutters. King's Chapel stood high like an empty ship, becalmed, balanced on the grass. Through Clifford's Court of Trinity we walked in ethereal light. Cambridge was nearly empty, most people had already gone down, but from some room somewhere about someone played a flute.

'Don't . . . tell anyone yet,' she had said.

'I shall tell them at once. Everyone.'

A weary-looking merrymaker in evening dress tottered from a doorway and blinked at the light. Charles said, 'Willie, I am about to be married.'

'Cheers,' said the reveller. He swung a champagne bottle by the neck, hands like a monkey, a glass in the other hand. 'Who's playing the bloody flute?'

'Listen—I am about to be married. May I introduce . . . ' but Ellie had gone on round the corner.

At breakfast before they went to the station his mother had been particularly charming to Ellie, seeing in her peaceful eyes gratitude for a lovely time. 'You will remember this all your life, my dear Ellie.' And Ellie had said yes. Oh yes. She would.

It was the next day in the green drawing-room of the Hall, when Charles and his mother were alone as she sat at her desk, that Charles had broken the news of his proposed future and all hell had broken loose.

# 19.

'It will be yours,' said Rosalie to Mr Drinkwater.

The Renoir had been secured in Drinkwater's easel and stood near the bed where she could see it close, leaving behind it, high on the wall, a pale patch of sunnier summer green than Rosalie would have believed possible. The room long ago must have been perfectly garish! Booth had supervised that frightful gardener this morning and there had been great play with a huge pair of steps which still stood in the room, giving it an air of removals. The two tall triangles of the steps and the heavy easel nearby were upsetting Drinkwater.

'Hope you're not thinking of spring-cleaning,' he said.

'Not just now.'

'No. Wouldn't be wise. Unseasonable. Too much for us all.'

'Yes. The Renoir, Edwin, is for you.'

'For me?' He went over and peered at it.

'When I die. I have left it to you.'

'Oh, no. No, no, no. Unnecessary.'

'You will sell it,' she said, 'or rather my lawyers will sell it for you if you need the money.'

'I'm quite well supplied,' he said. 'Quite adequately remunerated.' Peering close he said, 'It won't be worth much.'

'It is. Already. But one day it will be worth very much more. It is one of his best.'

'Don't like Renoir.'

'You're jealous.'

'Not at all. Fat girls. No. I don't want it. I'll have a Crome if there's one going.'

'You sound as if you're asking for a cream bun.'

'That's a cream bun.' He tapped the Renoir like a barometer.

'Rubbish! Don't you really want it? I could leave you . . . '

'Leave, leave! Pairs of steps. Removals. Spring-cleaning—where you going? Not realistic.'

'Realistic?'

'To talk of moving. In your condition.'

'I shall soon move, nevertheless.'

Prowling about the room Drinkwater said, 'Lear lived for years. Always falling about.'

'The king or the poet?'

'The painter. All of them. Same old joke.'

They laughed.

'You are a very clever man,' she said, 'but your brain hops too fast. Why don't you want the Renoir? You mean it?'

He examined the pale brocade of a curtain—pearl green. He took a rose from the buttonhole in his linen suit and held it against the brocade. The rose was peach-coloured. He moved the rose and held it against a blue silk chair. 'Either is good,' he said.

'There *is* a Crome.'

'Ah!'

'It was for Charles. All the pictures are for Charles except the Renoir, and the money—what's left and it won't be so bad—the money's for poor Binkie. Nobody else. Booth a thousand.'

'One in a thousand,' said Drinkwater.

'Let's hope so,' she said. 'Two would be terrible.' They laughed. She felt a heaviness in him after a moment as he wandered about. 'Are you all right? Have you a headache?'

'That girl—that child . . . '

'The little Renoir? What about her?'

'Could do with seeing her. Like to paint her. No Renoir. No cream-bun element. Bony. Never cared for jam puffs.' He shambled away behind her into the conservatory and Rosalie heard, with ears grown sharper as the rest of her faded, the slight movement of the door handle of the drawing-room and the door opening a jot. The hushed voices of Booth and the doctor were ending a conversation.

'Good gracious, the steps!' Booth cried out loudly as she came in, 'I'm sorry, doctor. The man should have taken them away.'

'I see the Renoir has approached,' said the doctor. 'Ha . . . yes. My word, it's very fine. I shouldn't move the steps, nurse. This should go back on high tonight. Or at any rate the windows ought to be locked.'

Rosalie said, 'I wanted to see it close again. But . . . '

The doctor looked at her. Then he said, 'Nurse, could you leave us please?' and Rosalie heard the crackle and bustle of Booth insulted fling out and the door close. She wondered if Booth would stand behind it listening and thought, probably not. The door is heavy. She must know by now that you could hear nothing. Where had she been while Drinkwater was in the room? She hoped well behind the shut door.

I forget everything else when I'm talking to Drinkwater she thought, except my delight in his madness. I've said unwise things. A thousand wouldn't be bad for Booth after hardly two years, but . . .

'What is it?'

The doctor stood where she would see him. She liked his sharp face and straight stare. He's ruthless and professional, she thought. He thinks I'm brave but he knows that I know it. He knows that I've a reputation. People disagree about me. I'm said to be hard. I was always thought vain. But he doesn't gossip about me—I'll put my head on the block to that. He knows there's nothing to be done for me but he doesn't just come for the whisky.

'I'm worse,' she said.

He said nothing.

'I can't . . . '

He waited.

'I'm beginning to find that I can't . . . '

'What?'

'See. I see double. Almost all the time now.'

'It's part of the complaint.'

'I've had it for a long time, but it is much worse. I . . . can't see the Renoir properly.'

'I'm afraid . . . ' he said, moving from beside the Renoir to his doctor's bag, opening it and taking out a stethoscope. 'Don't bother with that,' she said. 'It's my eyes. If my eyes go there is very little point . . . '

He did not try to disagree.

'I shan't last long,' she said. 'Now, thank God.'

He came over and held her twigs of hands. She said, 'Doctor . . . the Renoir . . . I want it to go to a girl . . . well, I suppose she's a woman now, Ellie—Elinor—I can't remember her other name. In the village. The mother kept the post office. Did you know them?'

'I'm afraid not. They are new people at the post office.'

'I don't know where she's gone. My son knew her. Could you make some . . . ?'

'Do you want me to see your son? Would you like to see your son here?'

She was quiet, thinking. He was still holding her hands as she dropped asleep.

# 20.

'Did he see you? Bezeer-Iremonger?'

'That's all you think of!'

'Well of course I do.'

'What I think of is . . . '

'Don't worry. I'll find you something of Binkie's.'

'I've no shoes. I can't wear Binkie's shoes. They're square. I couldn't lift them off the ground. He's insane—insane. Gassed in the War, my foot—he's a lunatic. He ought to be in your mother's Mental Home. And he's sinister—there's something odd about him.'

'Some slippers. I'll find some slippers. Maybe there's an old pair of slippers. Don't worry, Ellie—and a . . . wrap of some sort.'

'So I'm to walk the streets in slippers and a wrap. Down Seaview Villas. Except that I'm not going back there.' She swirled the bedcover round her and trailed over to the window with it flowing behind.

'Come away from the window,' he said fast.

'Why?' Far from turning she began to undo the catch and open it. Her big bare shoulders shone. Lifting both arms up she began to take long metal pins out of her hair. It dropped down lock by lock.

'Ellie,' he said, pulling her. 'Come here. Come away from the window. Someone passing . . . '

'What?' She turned and the bedcover slid down. He caught at it with a yelp. 'It's—the School. It wouldn't do me any good at the School.'

'You'd get sent to the Headmaster?' She laughed and walked across and touched his face and ran a finger across his mouth.

'You are so different, Ellie.'

'No.'

'You—you're making me different. You are making me . . . like you were.'

'Shy?' she said and clasped both arms round his neck. Over her shoulder he saw some people hurrying across the park. They looked like some of his boys. He saw what they saw: a big naked female back, one camisole strap hardly visible, flesh-coloured; long locks of hair on creamy shoulders and his own narrow, squirrelish face peeping over one of them. He tugged her away from the window and found that it was down on to the bed. She unclasped her hands in order to put both arms round his neck, to the elbow, climbed on top of him and shut her eyes. 'Ellie . . . ' He felt worse now, lying there with his shoes on, grey flannel bags and his old green cardigan. He felt his toes were sticking up in the air. Even with Ellie lying along him like a fallen statue on a bank he couldn't forget about shoes on the bed. Miss Pannell would have . . .

She was a heavy statue. Though softening and warm.

'Ellie . . . '

'Mmm?'

'We have to talk. Listen. What happened?'

But now she appeared to be sound asleep.

And it would be indecent, he thought, indecent of me not to make love to her. It would be wrong not to. She is back. I am forgiven. She intends it. She has taken charge.

And that is the trouble. She has taken charge. In the end even Ellie has taken charge of me. What is it in me which women are determined to command? It is because Ellie never commanded that I . . .

Yet he could not say 'I loved her' even now. For all the years of her absence he had assumed that he had loved her, had discovered it only when his mother had won the day. At first, after the débâcle and their flight to Devonshire it had not been so much like love as a haunting, a bird on the shoulder that would not fly away. Then later, with the work—teaching and books and years passing—her image had diminished—not exactly dimmed but hazed over a little, softened and sweetened. He never once had mentioned her to Binkie or on the one or two occasions when he had seen his mother again, and found self-respect of a kind in the fact that they were more shaken by silence than by any reproaches or signs of regret.

To Binkie it had been simple—clear from the start that he had done wrong to give the girl up. He had paid for it too—rejecting Ellie for an inheritance and then losing the inheritance in the subsequent quirk of Rosalie's turning the Hall over to a purpose which would suit her children's left-wing ways. But she had accepted that this was a fact, thinking that Charles was after all a weak man, easily fooled and in need of care. In his face she saw bland kindness rather than passion denied and assumed therefore that he suffered less than most. Sex (she held) was after all more necessary to the uneducated. By asserting that she herself needed sex less because of Cambridge she did in fact need it less. Girton—though not in any way romantic—had become the equivalent of romance and had grown with time softer and sweeter, rather as Ellie had become for Charles. She considered herself perfectly fulfilled in this physical department and her troubles now (she felt) had nothing to do with the lack of a man.

Charles however she believed to be in no particular need of fulfilment. He had always been quiet. In spite therefore of the specific twelve-year silence about Ellie she did not think it a brooding silence springing from any passionate source. He was witty company and very tidy and she continued to command him and he to think that Ellie's wish to be commanded had been the golden gift he had rejected and his great mistake.

All right then! Charles thought now, when he put his cardiganed arms awkwardly around her, over her warm smooth shoulders—when he had loved her . . .

As he still loved her.

The bird had not flown away.

He slid his fingers under the camisole strap and eased it off and Elinor sighed and moved her head against his neck and the last heavy locks of brown hair fell down over his hands.

And why at this moment did the room seem full of his upturned shoes, the toecaps erect and gleaming at the end of the bed, polished by Binkie this morning, the laces so neatly tied? I can see nothing else, he thought, nothing else—because I don't want to think: I don't want to recognise that this woman bears no resemblance whatsoever to the one I used to know. That one had been little and precise, withdrawn and self-conscious to the point of agony. Almost to invisibility. And inarticulate and very likely, which was what would have made it all possible, cold. For there had been nothing more physical than hand-holding in the years past, once or twice unsatisfactory kissing in Eastkirk woods, some dreaming about under the big sycamore down by the dry stream bed and the private bridge with the wicket gate. Well . . .

This woman now was—well, bold. And—well, shameless really.

And large.

He blinked again and swallowed, remembering that she had had a child two months ago. Yet here she was. And very heavy.

He moved out from underneath her, and she sighed as he began slowly to untie his shoelaces. He placed the shoes as he always did at night side by side at the end of the bed. He said, 'I think I'll lock the door.'

'Why? Nobody's here.'

'They might burst in.'

'Parsons, ironmongers,' she said, 'Binkie! Oh, I should like to see Binkie's face. Oh, don't look so *sad*!' She laughed and held out her arms.

And 'Charles,' she said afterwards, 'I'm glad.'

The window she had left unlatched suddenly blew open and banged to again. 'It's all right,' he said. 'It's just the wind.'

'But there is no wind. There's been no wind. The earth's—oh, Charles—stood still this summer.'

'It's over now,' he said. 'A storm coming.'

'Listen,' he said long afterwards. The window clattered again.

'It *is* a storm,' she said. 'A wind rising. That's why those people were hurrying crossing the park. Funny—nobody's been hurrying for months and months. I thought—I thought the heat would last forever. All those still days . . . '

'Stop talking,' he said.

'Oh, Charles—that's better. You're like you were.'

'At Queen's?'

'Oh no—much, much before that. You're as you were when we played on the Afghan rug.'

'This is better than an Afghan rug.' They lay peaceful as the wind blew nearer and nearer and battered against the house. It had grown quite dark. She said, 'I think there's going to be thunder.'

Rain splashed like hail on the glass and there was thunder. The window swung. Very far away there were some loud cracks like falling trees, or guns.

The narrow room, like the rest of the house, usually full of light till late evening, was now almost completely shadowed, and pulling the bedcover over themselves they lay in the twilight. The window swung again.

'I'd better get up and shut it,' he said but still did nothing.

Then way across the sandhills the loud crackling noises came again, each one preceded by a long fizzing explosion.

'Rockets,' he said. 'It's the lifeboat. Who'd have thought a storm would come up now? Someone must be in trouble on the rocks.'

# 21.

Lydia and Marsh did not hear Margaret pass the dining-room door, but ten minutes later did hear Elinor gasp and stumble as she passed and caught a flash of her staring face as she stood there, her mouth slightly open and ready to ask if someone would go and bring in Margaret from the beach.

Then she was gone, running, slamming the front door behind her. Lydia removed Marsh's hands, which had stayed frozen on her back, one of them by now inside her hooks-and-eyes. They were both standing pressed up between the wall and the corner of the knobbly sideboard, which had not been built for love.

Lydia turned and left the dining-room and went straight up to the top of the house to her own bedroom. It was a small room built out over the bathroom at the back and looked out through a scant net curtain on a string over the backyard and beyond to the few well-kept rows of vegetables and clumps of flowers. The one small fruit tree surprised her by suddenly shaking itself about, and she saw that the sky had changed and there were clouds. When Marsh followed her up to the door of her room she felt him there. They stood quite intent, Marsh breathing rather fast. 'Weather's gone then!' she said.

She heard him easing his feet about on the slip mat outside her door. He cleared his throat, and she leaned forward against the glass and rolled her head to let her cheek rest against it. 'Hadn't yer best git after 'er?'

The room, right up under the roof, had darkened fast and her big body blocking the window made it darker still. Behind her the hot room smelled fiercely of Lydia and Woolworth's scent. There was an iron bedstead, the curtain over the corner for her clothes and a cheap chest of drawers, mostly hanging open with clothing sticking out of them untidily. The dressing-table—an orange monster from some other sphere where it can never have been made much of—was thick with a dust of peach face-powder and a dirty, peach-coloured swansdown powder puff with a bedraggled blue ribbon lay there beside three or four orange and rose lipsticks. Bits and pieces of nameless things had been pushed under the swing mirror—hair-pins, cotton. A dirty brush and broken comb and a huge, sixpenny bottle of Devonshire Violets were muddled together with some giant metal hair-curlers, some spidery heaps of what might perhaps be hair-nets and some discarded puff-balls of hair. There was the Gladstone bag, one upright wooden chair and on the wall a picture of Jesus clinging to a precipice and with a free hand trying to catch hold of a substantial and unenthusiastic lamb. Above the bed was a text saying Feed my Sheep and propped on the dressing-table a big glossy photograph of Errol Flynn. The bed was narrow and high and sagged.

'You not been up 'ere.' Lydia was making a statement, not asking a question. 'Is it plain enough for yer? No temptations of the devil 'ere, is there? Or don't you like the look of Errol Flynn? Errol Flynn's about all there is of me own. The lambs and sheep is fixtures.'

Marsh held out his hands.

'There's me trunk undert bed and me bag. Them's me own, mind, and you can git gone while I packs them.'

She pulled the trunk out. It was a cardboard affair with poor brass clasps turning black, and plywood bands. Flinging it open she revealed a heap of dirty washing, which she crammed into a corner and then began to fling in clothes from the chest of drawers. Marsh shouted, furiously, 'You made me.'

She laughed, 'An't yer goin' after 'er? That's the first word you've spoke.'

He walked across and stood beside her as she knelt at the trunk, but she at once got up and began to walk frenziedly about, gathering up more clothes, her nightdress from under the pillow and an armful of things off the dressing-table. She hurled them all at the trunk and the scent of Devonshire Violets flooded through the room.

She was shaking. It might have been with tears, but when she knelt beside the trunk again and he put his hand on her hair she flung round and her great ramshackle face was not sad but furious.

'You near got me. D'you hear that? You damn near got me. Yer bringin' in the sheaves and God's love and all God's children has wings. Put yer burden on the Lord and all that muck. What Lord? What Lord?

'No Lord goes trampin' the mountains and woods after me. There's bin plenty others after me I'll tell yer sin I were eleven year old—our dad an' all. But no Lord. Our Dad layin' about the 'ouse all day, me Mam wi' eight on us an nowt but the dole. There was plenty after me an' none worth owt. None of them. An' I gets in to service at the last an' all's changed. Told there's love of me—more love than what's obvious. More to everythin' than what's obvious. More than food and drink and gettin' work and like you said. More to it than pickin' up what you can get where you can get it. You said. Being good, you said. Stoppin' sayin' yes every time. Withstanding temptation, sez you. Thinkin' of others sez you.

'Not that I ever did owt *but* think of others, seems to me. No chance of owt else in our 'ouse—me Mam useless, wore out and me Dad a devil and kids to get fed. To get to school even, some'ow. Some on them any rate. Him drunk Saturdays. Then drunk most other days and nowt left to eat in the end foreby fish an' chips if we's lucky.

'We'd not got lino on our kitchen floor. There now! Nowt but old boards. No bathroom. One lavvy for the street, down tother end ont railway bank. We'd o' bin hungry many an' many a time without me being round the pub of a night gettin' what I could get.

'So I comes 'ere—and that were a mystery; some mistake— an' it's all God's love. Four good meals a day. Easy, Easy. Train rides on a Wednesday to be comp'ny for a lass. A marriage as quiet and grand as in the *Woman's Weekly*. Jesus of Nazareth Sundays, an' prayers twice a day and thoughts all above the usual. Beautiful singing. Readings. People caring . . .

'You cared for me. That's what you said. You cared different. You was the daftest, differentest man I ever saw. Comin' out over them rocks after me in your smart clothes and there's nowt—not owt—distracts you, not even when I teks me stockin's off, not even when you falls down flat on yer face int' water. It wasn't me body you was after. Me body's not owt.

'Thinks I. *Thinks* I. Bloody great fool I is.

'Yer allt same. The bloody lot. There's not one man different. Yer face is poker straight and there's not a spark of desire about you an' it's back and forth yer go to that Bank day in day out an' off to yer Turner Street, steppin' out like Holy Jerusalem. But the same dirt's below—no better'n our Dad.

'Worse. A lot worse'n our Dad, seein' he'd all the excuse to go wrong as any man ever needed. Never a job in six years and me Mam wi' the face of a dead monkey an' kids wi' their noses runnin' and their mouths hangin', Bishop Auckland not bein' exactly the Garden of Eden you knows so much about.

'An so you should an all, livin' this place. Bloody seaside every day of your life an' not just for outin's. When I were a kid I never *seed* it but for twice on day-trips an then it was only Sea'ouses and bitter cold and windy and rain teeming down.

And you've got all this—all the grand sands and the waves runnin' in, as well as the woods an all—bands playin' people laughin' and spendin' money, singin' and dancin' and the chaos for the ice creams and the ladies in their 'ats that must have cost a good pound, and the red and blue flowers in the cut-out beds, and the blazing sunshine!'

She was sobbing into her hands but when he moved she jumped up and turned on him furiously.

'You an' yer Jesus Saves and all yer want is yer 'ands up me drawers the minute I gets near yer, stretching for fruit! You're the serpent, that's what you are Mr Holy Jesus Marsh, yer no God Almighty, yer the bloody serpent that had all the luck. Adam an' Eve gits kicked out, right? An' who stays back to enjoy it, eh? In the flamin' Garden of Eden? The serpent what was there from the start, from the first moment when He separates the light from the dark and the land from the sea an' starts messin' about wi' fishes. Like Margaret said, why din he stop there, wi' the light and the dark? The serpent won, din' he? An' there's trouble an' misery an' sex forever.'

She fastened the trunk clumsily, still crying, and threw herself on the sagging bed.

'So I can't stay 'ere. Can I? An' she'll give me no reference, so it's good-bye service an' back ont street corners. And God 'elp them kids—an' thy kids I mean, not me Dad's. Me Dad's kids'll make out best int' end, not bein' buggered up wi' Jesus.'

# 22.

When the rockets went up, Nurse Booth was spooning a second sugar into her tea, watched admiringly by Mabel Danby, the wife of the Chaplain, in the lodge at the gates of the Hall. The Danbys lived in the lodge and could see the Hall from it and the Chaplain was at present standing looking up the drive out of his sitting-room window at the curious darkening sky, and jingling the money in his pockets.

He was an immediate, enthusiastic man—the kind who comes up very close when he speaks, full of Welsh urgency and good will—but he thoroughly disliked Nurse Booth and was wondering whether the sudden rain and the threatening twilight sky were excuse enough for him to hear the call of duty and do a round of the wards.

'Gracious me—whatever's this,' he said.

'Thunder—well, I'm not surprised,' said Mabel, never taking her eyes off Booth. She passed a plate of little cakes across the dumb-waiter and Booth who was sitting knees-apart by the fireplace helped herself to a couple.

'Maids of honour,' said Mrs Danby.

'I sugar my tea,' said Booth. 'You can always tell a nurse by the sugar she puts in her tea.'

'Really,' said Mabel.

'We always said on the Somme, the better the tea the better the nurse. And the better the nurse the better the tea.' She looked round her for acclaim.

'Fancy.'

'My word, but it's a storm. It is a storm,' said the Chaplain. 'Now whoever would have thought at dinner time . . . '

'The only time I never drank tea,' said Booth, 'was in Singapore. And that's very funny really, very satirical, considering that Singapore is the home of tea.'

'Yes. Well of course. Why . . . ?'

'Too hot. Much too hot. The sweat poured from us. Poured from us. We drank water—plain water. Eight bottles a day.'

'Good heavens.'

'Mind, the food made up for it. Rice for breakfast of course. Great fat prawns.'

'Prawns, fancy!'

'That was lightning,' said the Chaplain, 'I wonder where Drinkwater is? He's not fond of lightning.'

'Not that you couldn't get an excellent steak and kidney pie.'

'More . . . er . . . tea, Evan?' Mabel Danby's big eyes asked her husband to turn round but he still jingled his pockets. Soon he began whistling through his teeth.

'In the Mess,' said Booth, 'you could get English cooking at its best. But out on the street stalls—the size of the prawns!' She lay back and opened her mouth and put into it a big piece of Sally Lunn. 'I always feel of course that one has never really lived unless one has been to the Far East.'

'Really.'

'Oh no.'

'I suppose not.'

'Never the same again. You're never the same again.'

'It must have been a great experience.'

'Oh yes. It spoils one. It rather spoils one. One tries not to be uppitty, but well, everywhere else feels a little bit of a comedown. I mean, Eastkirk and the Hall is such a very small pond.'

'It must be.'

'Poor Mrs F. One has to curb one's tongue a little. If she had travelled of course. You don't get this regal attitude in the ones who've been about a bit.'

There was a grinding, shuffling noise from the window.

'Abroad all the officers—are always so approachable. I only nursed officers of course.' Booth's stomach and great chest were as one, and though she was off-duty with no trace of starch, the spread from armpit to armpit cried out for medals. 'I was *Major* Booth then of course. I still take Major.'

Mabel, who had heard it all before, decided on a daring question.

'Didn't it . . . er . . . rather tend to sort of put the officers off?'

Booth looked hard at her and picked up a piece of Victoria Sponge. 'One thing I missed I really did miss,' she said kindly, 'and that was a real English tea. You could get it of course—Raffles, the Cricket Club . . . but . . . '

The rockets went off again and this time made Mabel jump.

'I think it's rockets,' she said.

'Rockets?'

'Rockets. Somebody in trouble.'

'And that of course,' said Booth munching, 'is another thing I miss here. The fireworks. The Chinese love fireworks, you know. They're an excitable people, excitable. Nonsense to say they're inscrutable. I understood them very well indeed. I felt really very close to the Chinese. I've a very good skin of course. And a flat back. And I love a bit of excitement—plenty going on. I suppose that's why I've never really hit it off in Eastkirk.'

The Chaplain put his head on one side rather in the manner of Mr Drinkwater, 'Sister . . . ' he began.

'Major,' she corrected, 'I still take Major.' She had become quite flushed with tea. 'You know I still like Major, Chaplain.'

'Major . . . Drinkwater. D'you think he'll be all right? He doesn't care for storms. D'you know where . . . ?'

'Oh, he'll be with Mrs F. Let's hope she'll decide to have the windows shut at last. Now don't you worry, Chaplain. Yes, just a small slice please—they're happy enough. The old love birds. Never fret.'

'Fret?' said the Chaplain. 'Fret? It's not *fret*.'

'Laughing away together. Of course she's getting as soft as him. I always say, you know, we'll all get the same way. Living here. They say that, don't they? You work in these places and you get just like them. One of the reasons I don't think I can see my way to staying very much longer.' She looked ruthlessly over at the Chaplain, 'It's you and me next, Evan.'

Mabel, astonished at the use of her husband's Christian name, laughed oddly and Booth began to twirl one of her feet and continued to look over at the Chaplain's back. Booth's eyes narrowed. 'Poor old virgin,' she said, and Mabel gasped.

'Nurse *Booth*! Mrs Frayling has two children . . . '

'Nothing to do with it!' said Booth largely. She flicked crumbs off her chest with short clean fingers. 'You can always tell,' she said, 'if you've been around a bit. *Unfulfilled*.' She leaned forward and nodded slowly. 'And dreaming half her life away. Fantasy world. Living in the past. Couldn't even keep peace with her children. That poor daughter comes . . . but the son never. Cut herself right off. It's what's known as a *Fantasy World*. Lives in the past. Mind she's lucky—she's lucky.'

'Lucky!'

'Oh yes. There's still money there. *Oh* yes!'

The rain began to slash down and blotted out the drive, the trees and the big, limp dahlias which the Chaplain and his wife grew devotedly in a cherry dump at the front door. They were meant to give a hopeful look to the mental-hospital gates and encourage the visitors. 'The dahlias will be quite dashed,' said Mabel.

'A bit of money makes *all* the difference.'

'Sorry. I'm off,' said the Chaplain, fled the room and returned buttoned up to the chin in his mackintosh and shaking out an umbrella. He kissed his wife, nodded towards Booth and said, 'Upsetting. Upsetting for Drinkwater. And some of the others. Mrs Frayling . . . '

'Now don't you worry about our Roaslie,' Booth called. (Rosalie! thought Mabel, Roasalie! She's drunk. Or is it the weather—there's a very queer light.) 'Our Rosalie's all right. No trouble to anybody if you mind your ps and qs and curtsey at the door. You'll not believe this but I like her. I really don't dislike her. It's—' she picked up a chocolate biscuit and looked at it, considering where to bite, 'It's always been a really nice case.'

'Nurse Booth,' shouted the Chaplain from the porch, letting the wind and rain blow in, 'if you will forgive me . . . ' His Welsh accent became strong when he was angry and his face if she had bothered to look up at it was as flushed as her own. 'I suggest you make the most of it because it will be a very short one now.'

'You don't need to tell me that, padre,' she said, leaning forward easily for sugar again and stirring. 'Not long now.'

The Chaplain left.

'I ought not to *say* this,' Booth looked up. 'I've never talked about a case. Never. I'm a professional—and of course a soldier. I ought not to say this . . . '

Mabel swallowed. 'A piece of Genoa?' she asked automatically. Then, torn between astonishment that Booth had accepted a large piece after so very much else, the horror at Booth's hypnotic, almost salacious excitement, she watched the nurse lick every finger-tip and at last say cunningly, 'About *three*, I'd say, Mabel. It'll be about three weeks.'

## 23.

Mrs Frayling heard the rockets too, but did not stir. Mr Drinkwater behind her in the conservatory heard them and cried out, 'Ship ahoy.'

He was sitting and listening to the noise in the near dark and to the rain, and watching the attack it made on the old green and black glass. Fusillades: yet they didn't seem to cut the roof moss. Outside green branches tossed in the greenish air.

Drinkwater sat in the splintery basket chair beneath the splintery vine and got wet from huge cold drops that fell on him through the cracks. There were holes to take glasses in the arms of the basket chair, but these were more like bird's nests. Mr Drinkwater was filling them with feathers from an old and hideous feather fan. The rockets added to the general feeling of eerie disturbance.

'Charles?' Rosalie called through.

'Ship on the rocks,' he called and shambled to Rosalie's room. She lay eyes-right on the pillow, thoughtfully. Her pil-low-case and counterpane shone blue-white in the dark room. Her tiny head looked darker and smaller than ever, a shrunk coconut, but her eyes were gigantic and bright.

'Not at all,' she said. 'The rockets are the sign for the lifeboat. Somebody is stuck on the rocks. There will be more in a minute. Wait and see. They signal twice to call the lifeboat men. In case they don't hear the first time. They all down tools and run. I saw them once. It's a good sight. Ancient.'

'Not a ship in distress?'

'No. I don't think so.' Her voice was surprisingly clear and firm and thoughtful.

'Magnificent sight—ship in distress.'

'You've never seen one, Charles.'

'No. Well—Turner. Van de Velde. Might just stroll down to the sea perhaps, if . . . ' He looked at her. 'I'm not Charles,' he said, ' . . . if you don't mind being left.'

'I am perfectly all right, but . . . '

'Don't care to leave you. Think I ought to stay about.'

'My dear Edwin—I am perfectly all right and how on earth do you think you could go out in this? You've always hated storms.'

Lightning lit the room and made the pillow dazzle round her face.

'Should care to paint you,' he said, then turned embarrassed to the open window. The world streamed and rattled with rain.

'Not allowed out anywhere, come to that,' he said, 'I've got me green ticket. That's what we used to say at the Slade—we're all going to finish with green tickets. That's what I've got.'

'What?'

'Not allowed to do anything,' he yelled. 'Can't hear meself speak either.'

'You're allowed to help me,' she said. 'Oh . . . !'

'What is it?'

Rosalie was looking beyond him and outside. Rain had soaked an arc in to the old green carpet inside the open french doors. One of the curtains lifted and dropped again, flapping. It had grown cold.

'I saw . . . '

'What is it?'

'A child. I saw a child looking in.'

Drinkwater peered about. 'Shut the window?' he asked. 'Better shut it now at last.'

'She didn't look like . . . '

'What?'

'She was different. Ill. Edwin—could you get Booth?'

'Booth?'

'Yes—quickly. Could you get Booth?'

'No children here,' he said, making a poor job of trying to close the French doors, rattling and bumping the closing bar and adding to the pandemonium of the rain.

'Stop it, Edwin—do leave me. But it was the same one.'

'What's that?' he said. He had begun to run a finger down the window then to place his hands on the pane and watch the warm marks they made fade when he had removed them. 'Same what?'

'It's the child we saw—we both saw—before. She's out there in the garden.'

'What child?'

'The child you were talking about.'

'I never saw a child. There's no child out there. The only child is here,' and he went over and tapped the Renoir head. 'Treacle sponge,' he said.

'There is a child in the garden, Edwin. Open the windows and call her.'

'There is a child in the garden,' said Drinkwater, leaning close to the painting, 'for ever in the garden. A fat meringue of a child, an éclair, profiterole, spun sugar and strawberry jam child. In a French garden. Thirty years ago. Not appealing. Now don't offer me it for Christsake. I don't want it.'

'I'm not talking about the picture. Edwin—please. Please . . . She's in the garden now. She must come in.'

'But she'd drown. She'd drown. Why should she be running about in the garden now? There's nobody in the garden now—not if they're in their right mind.' He peered at the picture and said, 'No more than there's anyone here.'

'She looked half-drowned,' said Rosalie, and felt a thundering and thumping in her chest, an awkward blundering beat and found she couldn't breathe easily. There was a terrible pain. When after a long time it passed she found—and it gave her more surprise than the pain which she had after all had sometimes before—she found that she was beginning to weep. As Drinkwater moved out of sight she got confused. 'Giles,' she called. The wounded Captain would have known what to do. He had understood her. Oh, the dreadful, shouting woman.

Yet he had gone away. He had let the shouting woman take him away. Suddenly a dazzlingly clear, almost luminous picture, like a picture at the edge of sleep, was in her head—the yattering little woman wrapping the wounded Captain in a rug, settling him in the back of a long, easy-looking motor car. Bobbing and frilly she bustled about. 'So kaind. So most awfully kaind'—and the car crackling slowly down the gravel drive and the Captain's head not once, not once, turning to look back as the car moved out past the lodge and through the gates and away south forever.

Standing back at the gate to allow the long car to pass had been Ellie. Ellie coming again—after quite an absence—to visit Charles, waving happily at Charles who went thankfully running to meet her, leaping down the steps where they had all been gathered to say good-bye, leaping, running, calling to Ellie who had come running forward to him.

Which was when I began to hate Ellie.

'Edwin,' she said, 'is there a desk?'

'Desk?'

'A little desk. Davenport. Somewhere about in the room.'

There were bumps and crashes. 'No.'

'Mother's desk. It must still be somewhere.'

'There's a *desk*. Yes—a desk. Sort of davenport thing I'd say. Behind the screen with all the jolly old water-slops.'

'Could you get a piece of paper—there should be pens . . . '

The rain streamed down the curtain. Far away a second lot of rockets sounded.

'Ha!' said Drinkwater. 'You were right.'

The pain closed over Rosalie's chest again, now like a fist. Drinkwater scuffled. 'A pretty pen,' he said, 'here in the little side drawer. Pretty paper. Thick as cloth. Do you feel like writing a letter then, Rosalie?'

'Write,' she said with difficulty. 'Write "For Ellie."'

He wrote slowly, sitting at the davenport among the medicine bottles and pillboxes, bed-pan and feeding cups and wrinkled damp flannels. The top of the davenport sloped. Its panel of old gold leather was uneven and scarred and the pen had a rusty nib, but he wrote in beautiful copper-plate with a mixture of spit and black dust from the misted brass and glass inkwell.

Rosalie was silent and he put his bearded face round the screen. His eyes grew rounder at her stillness and what looked like a dark little metal claw which clutched the sheet. 'On the picture,' however she said clearly. 'Put it on the picture. "For Ellie."'

'Ellie who?'

'For . . .' There was such a pause that Drinkwater's mind wandered. The wind and the rain, he thought, the rockets and the storm. Child in the garden. Ridiculous, child in the garden. Not likely in the least. Then he too seemed to see a child run across the wild wet garden, very small like a blown leaf.

'Put "For Ellie",' said Rosalie,' '"the child who visits the garden".'

'Well, maybe, maybe not,' said Drinkwater and wrote, 'For Ellie—the child who visits the garden', and he propped the note on the Renoir. 'For all we know there may be two or three of them,' he said, and turned and patted Rosalie's hand. It was not now clutched like a claw but still, and she was looking quietly and steadily out through the open window.

'Speak to Booth,' he said. 'Get that filthy fool Booth. Witnesses. Notes and legacies no good without witnesses. I'm no witness. Mad as a hare. Or that's what they think. Dare say they're right.'

The Chaplain bounced in through the windows shaking an umbrella. 'Good God, Drinkwater, shut these.'

'Likes them open.' Drinkwater was red in the face. 'Can't hear meself speak.' Tears were in his eyes and he was shouting.

'Dare say not. Calm down, man. What's all this! What's this document on the picture? Now then what have the two of you been up to? What have you been up to, Mrs Frayling?'

Then after a moment by the bed he turned and said to Drinkwater, 'All right, Edwin. All right, old chap. Don't cry. Go and get Booth.'

# 24.

'And then,' said Binkie, buttering fish-paste rolls and crossing her ankles which stuck out of old ARP trousers, 'and then,' raising her voice against the seagulls, 'your father and one of his friends rushed to the lifeboat house, where the doors were just opening and the men pushing it out. Your father wasn't a lifeboatman—his friend may have been, I think. He was a bit of everything, Mr Bezeer—your father was only a bank manager. But he was very, very brave. He insisted, *insisted* on going aboard the boat. He kept shouting and everyone said that it wasn't a bit like him. He never showed his feelings except in church—he was the other way round from most of us—he kept on shouting, "It is my daughter, my daughter, on the rocks." No prayers—just that.'

'Didn't the lifeboatmen . . .' Terence paused. Binkie passed him a fish-paste roll and he opened his mouth to bite it and then put it down on the grass. Eating rolls as you hear details for the first time of the death of your father seemed bad. Even if you had never known him.

'Is somethin' wrong with it?' asked Binkie. 'Fish paste?'

'No—just while you were telling me, about . . . well, how he drowned.' His younger brother Alfred munched on. Binkie said, 'Alfred doesn't mind.'

'You shouldn't have told him it was fish,' said Alfred.

'Shut up,' said Terence. 'What I mean is—well, didn't the lifeboatmen just sort of kick him out of the way? I mean they wouldn't be allowed to let just anyone in. Was he huge?'

'He was a very small man, a neat little man. Rather as you will be, Terence. I never knew him of course. I only saw him sometimes from a distance preaching on the sands. A very small man, but with great power. He gathered crowds, you know. I always imagine him to have been something rather like St Paul.'

'Was he a nutter?' asked the younger brother, taking a third roll. 'They say he was a nutter.' He was a tall boy, much bigger than his brother though over eleven months younger.

'He believed in his Mission,' said Binkie. 'At home I understand he was very silent. But the story goes that he became frantic, *frantic* at the lifeboat house and somehow got on board. And of course, knowing nothing about ships and storms, he was the one swept off and drowned. So was the friend, poor Mr Bezeer. The lifeboatman. But he had been gassed.'

'Gassed! On the lifeboat?' Binkie gave Alfred a long glare.

'That doesn't sound much like St Paul anyway,' said Terence. 'St Paul told the sailors what to do.'

'Perhaps my father tried to,' said Alfred. 'Maybe he started bossing and they didn't like it. Maybe they just went swoosh.'

Binkie looked at the pair of them and then leaned back against the monument. It was a squat little black monument with the names of the drowned men cut in shiny new gold letters. The grass had not yet grown up around it again, like a new grave, and the sandy soil was trampled about by yesterday's ceremony.

It had been called an unveiling though Mabel Danby and the Chaplain who had given the tea afterwards and been a great support all day had said that this was ridiculous. You cannot unveil a stump. 'Stumps,' had said Nurse Booth, who had turned up unexpectedly and made herself very agreeable—she had been dressed in khaki with the insignia of a nursing field marshal—'Stumps cannot be curtained.' Similar memorials in the Western Desert, she had said, had always been established by the firing of cannon, and Alfred who had said that he didn't see how you could have monuments to shipwrecks in the Western Desert had been ignored, Booth only glaring at him now and then during the singing of 'For those in Peril' by the Eastkirk branch of the British Legion, the RNLI, the Mayor and corporation, a man with a large head who clinked a bag and some members of ever-surviving Turner Street.

The whole occasion had in fact been difficult from start to finish, not least because after talking of the monument for three years after the event, the War had come and put if off for another six, and the cliff-top declared out of bounds for other, and bigger potential shipwrecks. Now, two more years later, the thing had been done at last in a rush, for development was threatened along the cliffs—and big things promised to restore the coastline below them. Already the Hall woods had gone and a maze of roads and little pink houses was growing to waist height all over what had been the Valley Gardens and the swell of the old great lawns. There was to be a funfair where the Hall had stood. Miles of black barbed wire were being cleared from the beaches below and some soldiers even as Binkie and Terence and Alfred picnicked were completing the demolition of the pier which had been put out of action eight years before to deter invaders. Alfred turned on his stomach now and watched a large piece of pier—part of a pretty wooden theatre—tilt and flap. Some frail cries came up from below and the whole thing slid down. Big light flakes of wood fell into the sea.

'Why are they doing it, Auntie Binkie?'

'Binkie,' she said, 'just Binkie. I'm not your aunt. I am a family friend. As a family friend I thought you should come to the unveiling and as a family friend I am giving you a picnic and having you to stay.'

'I always thought you were Margaret's aunt.'

'If I were Margaret's aunt I would be your aunt. But I knew Margaret when she was only eight. You are her brothers. I am nobody's aunt.'

'Before she nearly got drowned? You knew her?'

'Yes.'

'You must have been pleased she hadn't got drowned?'

'Yes.'

'In fact I expect it was quite a shock she hadn't got drowned, wasn't it? When even lifeboatmen did?'

'Yes.'

'She climbed the cliff, didn't she? This cliff.' Terence wormed to the edge of it and looked over. 'Crikey!' Alfred worming up beside him said, 'I could of. Couldn't you?'

'Don't know. She's funny, Margaret. She looks too sort of quiet to climb a thing like this.'

'You don't have to be noisy to climb cliffs. She got cut off by the tide so she just had to. She's awfully dreamy, Margaret. But she can do things sometimes.'

'Binkie'—Terence turned round—'Binkie, what exactly happened? That friend, the one who got drowned too. With the funny wife who came to unveil the monument?'

'Here comes Margaret,' said Binkie. The three of them watched an uncertain-looking girl of twenty wandering about in the foundations of the new house below where the cliff sloped down inland to what had been the woods. 'Funny woman? You mean Mrs Bezeer? Well, she was just the wife of Mr Bezeer. He had a very important sort of name, Mr Bezeer-Iremonger, and well, he was a little . . . just a little . . . '

'His wife was a little, too,' said Alfred. Both boys rolled about snorting on the grass. Although so different in character and appearance, so that it was forever being said that nobody would ever take them for brothers and was it not interesting how posthumous children so seldom resembled the father—although they were so different, Terence and Alfred got on very well.

'Mrs Bezeer,' said Binkie sternly, 'had a terrible life. Terrible. One must be very sorry for Mrs Bezeer. And tolerant.'

'How pompous old Binkie is,' Margaret thought, coming up towards them and flopping down on the grass. 'She's got portentous. I suppose you . . . '

'Paste sandwich, Margaret?' Binkie looked over her glasses. 'Where've you been? We've been talking about Mrs Bezeer and her sad life.'

'Thanks. Why sad? She's a dreadful woman, isn't she? She flutters and shrieks and fusses. She's all bangles. Says "fraightfully". She's all over the place.'

'So would you be if you'd been married to Mr Bezeer. Now he was all over the place. Literally. Don't you remember him? All over the place. Round every corner. Cropped up everywhere.'

'I think he once told me to get off a seat,' said Margaret. 'Something about hating me. Hating everything. He dribbled or something.'

'He grew to dribble. Not at first. He was shell-shocked you know. In the First War. He was still, even after his injuries, the most delightful, most peaceful sort of man at first, but in time quite destroyed. He was sent up here to recover. He was a patient as a matter of fact at the Hall when I was a girl. Where I grew up. Only the lodge left now. I remember him. He didn't dribble then. He sat all day on the terrace and stared into space. He was very good-looking. I was a bit in love with him. He was not unlike'—she busied herself with Thermos flasks—'not unlike Father Carter.'

'What happened after that,' Margaret asked, sipping China tea, 'exactly?'

'I don't quite know.'

'Charles would say, "Then what happened *in*exactly."'

'I don't know inexactly. Something must have done. He got much worse. My mother used to sit with him on the terrace sometimes all day long but they hardly spoke. Mother was always a bit frightening. You know—very tall. Like old Queen Mary. The army nurses used to say she used to scare him. It was rather awful. Then Mrs Bezeer came one day to take him home—such a pretty little thing. Just the same as she is now and it's over twenty-five years. Very brave and jolly and affectionate—a bit chatty, but a good little woman. He hardly seemed to know she was even there. He *looked* perfectly normal—well, very much so. A lovely, romantic Galahad sort of face—but he never said one word. The day she got him—Mrs Bezeer—into the car to take him back to Surrey—she was a Guildford woman, I believe—he just stared straight in front of him. My mother and all of us were on the steps. He never even said good-bye. Mrs Bezeer turned to thank Mother, but Mother—well of course, Mother was a snob. She was a bit of a joke really but nobody minded. She belonged to the past. But, oh yes—a fearful snob. I don't think she had ever heard of Guildford and she turned away and stood with her back to us all until the car passed. I must say Mrs Bezeer took it very well. But there was a frightful atmosphere.'

'I expect she was very grateful really,' said Terence.

'Probably the man just couldn't feel able to say the right thing,' said Alfred. 'People aren't.'

'You may be right,' said Binkie. 'Your mother said . . . well, your mother was just a girl. She used to come up to see us a good deal. She said—she was standing at the gate that day. She hadn't been to see us for some time. The car passed her with the Bezeers in it—your mother, Ellie, said that Mrs Bezeer was talking very fast and determinedly and nod-nodding at the Captain—he was a Captain, I've just remembered—at Captain Bezeer, and Captain—it was Miles—Miles no *Giles* Bezeer was quite, quite silent, but he was crying. Crying—tears running all down his face. And a Captain!'

'But he went to Surrey,' said Terence after a bit. Margaret put her fingers in the gold lettering of the stump and felt the name of Giles Bezeer-Iremonger whom she had killed.

'Well,' said Binkie, 'a few years later he reappeared in the town. Though he looked quite different. He was all alone. He took lodgings somewhere, not near the Hall, nearer where you all lived—Seaview Villas way. We were not here then—Charles and I moved away for a time. We didn't move back until you were about eight years old, Margaret. You will remember. People do tend to move back here—and our mother was dying by then. By the time we came back and bought the house in Dene Close, there was this funny, dirty quite old-looking man roaming about. I sometimes thought he reminded me of someone, but he was very changed and the name didn't ring a bell. Perhaps I'd only heard of him as "the Captain" when I was a girl. He used to push a little cart about the sands and he haunted all the churches. He gathered wood and seacoal. The wife had quite vanished. Then your father took him in hand and got him singing.'

'Singing?' said Alfred. Terence rolled.

'Yes. Hymns. He grew very devout. I don't think there was a religion here he didn't take up at one time or another.'

'Sounds as if everyone was a bit potty round here,' said Terence, 'in those days. They're not so potty now are they? Maybe this last war cleared the air a bit.'

'Did he never go back to the Hall?' Alfred chewed grass.

'I don't think so. But he used to wander about the woods sometimes. Yes—I think he may have done odd jobs there, even. But Mother grew very strange, you know. Not many people went back to see her. I don't think they met again.'

'The Hall's gone now,' said Margaret, 'I've been to see. They're going to build over where the woods were. A new town or something. They've kept the lodge though.'

'Yes.' Binkie and Margaret smiled at each other. Binkie said, 'And put up the blue plaque.'

'"Edwin Drinkwater, painter, at one time lived near this house."'

'I wish you'd known him, Margaret.'

'I did.'

'No, dear, you couldn't. He was quite ga-ga by the time you were born. More or less under lock and key—though he improved when he came to live with us at the end. He didn't live very long after Mother.'

'I did. I did know him.'

'I expect your mother told you about him.'

'She never knew him. I did. He used to talk while he painted. Very hot days in summer.'

'I expect that was a dream. The days in summer always seemed very hot when we were children. Somebody must have told you about him.'

'He wore wellingtons,' said Margaret.

'I don't see that that's so marvellous,' said Terence.

'It shows it can't have been that hot,' said Alfred.

'He painted snakes.'

'Yes,' said Binkie. 'Yes—that is true. He did paint snakes at one stage. Not at the end—his last pictures were quite different. Just big quiet blocks of colour. Charles—my brother—you don't know Charles, you boys—Charles and I loved them. He did them when he lived with us at Dene Close, before he died. Charles has quite a few of them—he took them with him to Australia.'

'I've seen some. In galleries,' said Margaret.

'Even the snake pictures are valuable now of course—and the early landscapes of Greece are treasures. They're said to be better than Lear's.'

'Who's Lear,' said Terence. 'Thought he was a king.'

'Charles would have loved to have one of those.'

'It's a shame Charles wasn't here yesterday,' said Margaret, 'for the unveiling.'

'It's a pity your mother wasn't here,' said Binkie. 'It was very much noticed, I'm afraid.'

'You know Mother,' said Margaret. 'Insisted we all come and then said that it would be impossible for her to leave Father Carter. She's so mad on the parish. She's parson's wife of parsons' wives. Albs and cottas. She's so—*excessive*. Though nice,' she added.

Binkie looked at Margaret and said, 'For a child of twenty you are ancient at times.'

'You ought to have been the parson's wife, Binks. It was you who should have married Father Carter. He'd have liked it better in the end. Poor ma. She's—oh, *tremulous*. She's like the famous Renoir. Over the sitting-room fireplace. Oh my!'

'The Girl in the Garden,' said Alfred. 'People come to the door to see it all the time. We're going to charge them soon, Mother says, it's to go to the stained glass restoration fund.'

'The Girl in the Garden,' said Binkie. 'I wonder what they would say to that in Turner Street? Your mother was solidly behind Turner Street once, you know, you children. For years. Unswervingly. Naked and unadorned.'

'That must have been pretty disgusting.'

'Not your mother naked and unadorned. Her view of God was naked and unadorned. The Saints let nothing distract from the source of light. No stained glass there.'

'Father Carter's not so keen on the stained glass either. Not as much as Ma now,' said Margaret. 'And he hates that boy with his mouth open over the grapes on the marble plinth you gave him. Says it looks ridiculous in Stepney. He's all right, Father Carter. You were the one for him though, Binks.'

Binkie said that it had been a great surprise to everyone that Father Carter had married at all, he was so High, and the two boys fell about again at this. Then they wandered away to throw stones down at the sea, which whispered faintly back at them. Binkie and Margaret ate biscuits and were quiet.

*

Margaret said at last, 'Tell me about her. Mother. That day.'

Binkie said nothing.

'There's a mystery of some sort, isn't there? About that day?'

'Which day?' Binkie asked, several moments later.

'The day I . . . climbed the cliff. Got stuck out on the . . . The day Father—I can't remember.'

'The day you can remember but won't.'

'I was only eight.'

'Which means nothing.'

'I know that. But it's my business. At least it's other people's, not mine. Their business to tell me.'

'No. It's other people's business, but not to tell you. I can't be the one to talk to you about your mother.'

'There was some sort of talk about her being wild in some way that day. In some way disgusting.'

'Disgusting?'

'Well—running about the beach with no clothes on or something.'

'Oh, Margaret! How ridiculous!'

'Don't put on your Girton voice, Binks. What was it? It's what I heard anyway.'

'Whoever . . . ?'

'I don't know. Rumours. That fat woman with the chest and the medals who was at the unveiling.'

'Booth? Sister Booth? She never knew your mother. Or you.'

'Yes—she did know me. They took me—afterwards. I got to the Hall in the rain. They took me into the lodge. She was there. She was rather a frightening woman. I'd seen her once before.'

'What rubbish! You are like Charles with your ideas of figures of doom.'

'But there was something, Binkie. And Charles going away. We never saw him again. We went away. Then he went away. What was it all about?'

Binkie thought of Ellie's curious pale green stockings among the clothes for the jumble sale, and Ellie's bare legs under Charles's old mackintosh as they huddled later in the tearing rain on the beach. She considered and dismissed, as she had often done before, the sloping shoulders of the child Alfred she so loved. She thought again of the long black gleaming slope of shale, the razor-tooth against which the lifeboat had ground and butted and foundered; of the bodies of poor old Bezeer and little limp Kenneth Marsh washed up three days later far down the coast at Flamborough. 'Do you keep up your Latin, Margaret?' she said.

'Yes. Of course. I have to.'

'Well yes, I suppose so, reading History. You're very like Charles, you know. I think of you sometimes as Charles's child.'

'Not Alfred?'

They looked at each other. 'I am my father's child,' said Margaret. 'D'you remember how I once knew the whole Bible backwards and inside out.'

'You were considered a miracle,' said Binkie. 'It's amazing how you can teach babies tricks. You were the Miracle of Turner Street—and of Dene Close, too. And I dare say of Seaview Villas. We were all terrified of you.'

'I was father's miracle,' said Margaret. 'He was awful—awful, but he had the most tremendous sort of power, Binkie. You didn't know him. Mother used to cry—and the house sort of . . . twanged. But he left me with a sense of God, Binkie. It is a big present.'

'I can imagine. But—Latin. Margaret, you know the verb exquire? To search out? To elucidate?'

'Yes.'

'Well, when I'm dead could you put it on my tombstone?'

'Yes.'

'With a non in front of it?'

'Yes. Why?'

'Because there's a lot it's not wise to fuss over. To prise out. Extract. It is best just to look and be.'

The boys were talking now to someone they had met up with a little distance along the cliff—a woman who had been at the unveiling but whom nobody had seemed to know—for Margaret had at the last minute not been present yesterday. She had been walking about the woods as she had been again today, and everybody had kindly understood. The woman, coming towards them now up the hill, was immense, with a floury powdered face and great bush of very golden fizz for hair. She was wearing a tight dress of purple satin and not quite white gloves and her shoes which had heels like spindles were taking badly to the sandy cliff-top. She was broad-shouldered and haunched like a ploughman, and no longer young, but the two twelve-year-old boys had fallen in step one on either side of her and were both looking up into her face with great attention as they all drew near. It looked like the approach of old and loving friends.

Lydia reached the monument with them and looked down at Binkie and the tall girl. 'Hullo, our Margaret,' she said and sat down. 'I's clemmed.'

'You ought to take your shoes off,' said Terence. 'They're not very suitable.'

'That's nowt new. I were never a great one for choosing right. Mind, I've 'ad me shoes off afore today—and not that far from 'ere. Trouble is, these days I'd nivver get 'em back on again.

'The tree's still there,' she said to Margaret, 'with the hole for me corsets. They're going to build round it—what about that?'

'Introduce me to your friend,' said Binkie.

'It's Lydia,' Margaret said and nothing more.

'Yer not that much different, our Margaret.'

'Will you,' asked Binkie, 'er . . . have a fish-paste roll?'

'No thanks. Yer taller, that's all.'

'You're not much different either, Lydia,' said Margaret.

From below the soldiers' cries wavered up unevenly on the wind. They were dragging out the great black hoops of wire which has been sunk deep in the sands all the War. The soldiers' little bodies were like insects running, in strings and groups. Slowly, unwillingly and painfully, the old wire was dragged away from the shifting drifts of white sand and far above, even the picnic party on the cliff-top, the seagulls sent other uneven calls down again, tilting, watching on the wind, tipping and gliding, sometimes skimming level with the grass, high out over the waves, their eyes brilliant and black, seeing what it was urgent for them to see, unconcerned with what was urgent and mutable for men.

'What did you do all the War, Lydia?'

'I lived on at Bishop. I were in munitions. Mekkin bombs.'

'Did you never marry?'

'Nivver. I'm not that daft.' She leaned her big head back and watched the seabirds. 'In't they bonny?' she asked Binkie.

'What?' asked Binkie, peering up.

'Yon,' said Lydia.

'You haven't changed either,' said Margaret with love. 'Not a bit.'

'Oh, our Margaret, but I have,' said Lydia, 'I were bloody daft them days.'

## About the Author

Jane Gardam is the only writer to have been twice awarded the Whitbread Prize for Best Novel of the Year (for *The Queen of the Tambourine* and *The Hollow Land*). She also holds a Heywood Hill Literary Prize for a lifetime's contribution to the enjoyment of literature.

She has published four volumes of acclaimed stories: *Black Faces, White Faces* (David Higham Prize and the Royal Society for Literature's Winifred Holtby Prize); *The Pangs of Love* (Katherine Mansfield Prize); *Going into a Dark House* (Silver Pen Award from PEN); and most recently, *Missing the Midnight*.

Her novels include *God on the Rocks* (shortlisted for the Booker Prize), *Faith Fox, The Flight of the Maidens* and *Old Filth*, a *New York Times* Notable Book of the Year.

Jane Gardam lives with her husband in England

**Carmine Abate**
*Between Two Seas*
"A moving portrayal of generational continuity."
—*Kirkus*
224 pp • $14.95 • 978-1-933372-40-2

**Salwa Al Neimi**
*The Proof of the Honey*
"Al Neimi announces the end of a taboo in the Arab world: that of *sex!*"
—*Reuters*
144 pp • $15.00 • 978-1-933372-68-6

**Alberto Angela**
*A Day in the Life of Ancient Rome*
"Fascinating and accessible."
—*Il Giornale*
392 pp • $16.00 • 978-1-933372-71-6

**Muriel Barbery**
*The Elegance of the Hedgehog*
"Gently satirical, exceptionally winning and inevitably bittersweet."
—Michael Dirda, *The Washington Post*
336 pp • $15.00 • 978-1-933372-60-0

*Gourmet Rhapsody*
"In the pages of this book, Barbery shows off her finest gift: lightness."
—*La Repubblica*
176 pp • $15.00 • 978-1-933372-95-2

www.europaeditions.com

**Stefano Benni**
*Margherita Dolce Vita*
"A modern fable…hilarious social commentary."—*People*
240 pp • $14.95 • 978-1-933372-20-4

*Timeskipper*
"Benni again unveils his Italian brand of magical realism."
—*Library Journal*
400 pp • $16.95 • 978-1-933372-44-0

**Romano Bilenchi**
*The Chill*
120 pp • $15.00 • 978-1-933372-90-7

**Massimo Carlotto**
*The Goodbye Kiss*
"A masterpiece of Italian noir."
—*Globe and Mail*
160 pp • $14.95 • 978-1-933372-05-1

*Death's Dark Abyss*
"A remarkable study of corruption and redemption."
—*Kirkus* (starred review)
160 pp • $14.95 • 978-1-933372-18-1

*The Fugitive*
"[Carlotto is] the reigning king of Mediterranean noir."
—*The Boston Phoenix*
176 pp • $14.95 • 978-1-933372-25-9

(with Marco Videtta)
*Poisonville*
"The business world as described by Carlotto and Videtta in *Poisonville* is frightening as hell."
—*La Repubblica*
224 pp • $15.00 • 978-1-933372-91-4

**Francisco Coloane**
*Tierra del Fuego*
"Coloane is the Jack London of our times."—Alvaro Mutis
192 pp • $14.95 • 978-1-933372-63-1

**Giancarlo De Cataldo**
*The Father and the Foreigner*
"A slim but touching noir novel from one of Italy's best writers in the genre."—*Quaderni Noir*
144 pp • $15.00 • 978-1-933372-72-3

**Shashi Deshpande**
*The Dark Holds No Terrors*
"[Deshpande is] an extremely talented storyteller."—*Hindustan Times*
272 pp • $15.00 • 978-1-933372-67-9

**Helmut Dubiel**
*Deep In the Brain: Living with Parkinson's Disease*
"A book that begs reflection."—*Die Zeit*
144 pp • $15.00 • 978-1-933372-70-9

**Steve Erickson**
*Zeroville*
"A funny, disturbing, daring and demanding novel—Erickson's best."
—*The New York Times Book Review*
352 pp • $14.95 • 978-1-933372-39-6

**Elena Ferrante**
*The Days of Abandonment*
"The raging, torrential voice of [this] author is something rare."
—*The New York Times*
192 pp • $14.95 • 978-1-933372-00-6

*Troubling Love*
"Ferrante's polished language belies the rawness of her imagery."
—*The New Yorker*
144 pp • $14.95 • 978-1-933372-16-7

*The Lost Daughter*
"So refined, almost translucent."—*The Boston Globe*
144 pp • $14.95 • 978-1-933372-42-6

**Jane Gardam**
*Old Filth*
"Old Filth belongs in the Dickensian pantheon of memorable characters."
—*The New York Times Book Review*
304 pp • $14.95 • 978-1-933372-13-6

*The Queen of the Tambourine*
"A truly superb and moving novel."—*The Boston Globe*
272 pp • $14.95 • 978-1-933372-36-5

*The People on Privilege Hill*
"Engrossing stories of hilarity and heartbreak."—*Seattle Times*
208 pp • $15.95 • 978-1-933372-56-3

*The Man in the Wooden Hat*
"Here is a writer who delivers the world we live in…with memorable and moving skill."—*The Boston Globe*
240 pp • $15.00 • 978-1-933372-89-1

**Alicia Giménez-Bartlett**
*Dog Day*
"Delicado and Garzón prove to be one of the more engaging sleuth teams to debut in a long time."—*The Washington Post*
320 pp • $14.95 • 978-1-933372-14-3

*Prime Time Suspect*
"A gripping police procedural."—*The Washington Post*
320 pp • $14.95 • 978-1-933372-31-0

*Death Rites*
"Petra is developing into a good cop, and her earnest efforts to assert her authority…are worth cheering."—*The New York Times*
304 pp • $16.95 • 978-1-933372-54-9

**Katharina Hacker**
*The Have-Nots*
"Hacker's prose soars."—*Publishers Weekly*
352 pp • $14.95 • 978-1-933372-41-9

**Patrick Hamilton**
*Hangover Square*
"Patrick Hamilton's novels are dark tunnels of misery, loneliness, deceit, and sexual obsession."—*New York Review of Books*
336 pp • $14.95 • 978-1-933372-06-

**James Hamilton-Paterson**
*Cooking with Fernet Branca*
"Irresistible!"—*The Washington Post*
288 pp • $14.95 • 978-1-933372-01-3

*Amazing Disgrace*
"It's loads of fun, light and dazzling as a peacock feather."
—*New York Magazine*
352 pp • $14.95 • 978-1-933372-19-8

*Rancid Pansies*
"Campy comic saga about hack writer and self-styled 'culinary genius' Gerald Samper."—*Seattle Times*
288 pp • $15.95 • 978-1-933372-62-4

*Seven-Tenths: The Sea and Its Thresholds*
"The kind of book that, were he alive now, Shelley might have written."
—*Charles Spawson*
416 pp • $16.00 • 978-1-933372-69-3

**Alfred Hayes**
*The Girl on the Via Flaminia*
"Immensely readable."—*The New York Times*
164 pp • $14.95 • 978-1-933372-24-2

**Jean-Claude Izzo**
*Total Chaos*
"Izzo's Marseilles is ravishing."—*Globe and Mail*
256 pp • $14.95 • 978-1-933372-04-4

*Chourmo*
"A bitter, sad and tender salute to a place equally impossible to love or leave."—*Kirkus* (starred review)
256 pp • $14.95 • 978-1-933372-17-4

*Solea*
"[Izzo is] a talented writer who draws from the deep, dark well of noir."
—*The Washington Post*
208 pp • $14.95 • 978-1-933372-30-3

*The Lost Sailors*
"Izzo digs deep into what makes men weep."—*Time Out New York*
272 pp • $14.95 • 978-1-933372-35-8

*A Sun for the Dying*
"Beautiful, like a black sun, tragic and desperate."—*Le Point*
224 pp • $15.00 • 978-1-933372-59-4

**Gail Jones**
*Sorry*
"Jones's gift for conjuring place and mood rarely falters."
—*Times Literary Supplement*
240 pp • $15.95 • 978-1-933372-55-6

**Matthew F. Jones**
*Boot Tracks*
"A gritty action tale."—*The Philadelphia Inquirer*
208 pp • $14.95 • 978-1-933372-11-2

www.europaeditions.com

**Ioanna Karystiani**
*The Jasmine Isle*
"A modern Greek tragedy about love foredoomed and family life."
—*Kirkus*
288 pp • $14.95 • 978-1-933372-10-5

*Swell*
"Karystiani movingly pays homage to the sea and those who live from it."
—*La Repubblica*
256 pp • $15.00 • 978-1-933372-98-3

**Gene Kerrigan**
*The Midnight Choir*
"The lethal precision of his closing punches leave quite a lasting mark."
—*Entertainment Weekly*
368 pp • $14.95 • 978-1-933372-26-6

*Little Criminals*
"A great story…relentless and brilliant."—*Roddy Doyle*
352 pp • $16.95 • 978-1-933372-43-3

**Peter Kocan**
*Fresh Fields*
"A stark, harrowing, yet deeply courageous work of immense power and magnitude."—*Quadrant*
304 pp • $14.95 • 978-1-933372-29-7

*The Treatment and the Cure*
"Kocan tells this story with grace and humor."—*Publishers Weekly*
256 pp • $15.95 • 978-1-933372-45-7

**Helmut Krausser**
*Eros*
"Helmut Krausser has succeeded in writing a great German epochal novel."—*Focus*
352 pp • $16.95 • 978-1-933372-58-7

**Amara Lakhous**
*Clash of Civilizations Over an Elevator in Piazza Vittorio*
"Do we have an Italian Camus on our hands? Just possibly."
—*The Philadelphia Inquirer*
144 pp • $14.95 • 978-1-933372-61-7

**Lia Levi**
*The Jewish Husband*
"An exemplary tale of small lives engulfed in the vortex of history."
—*Il Messaggero*
224 pp • $15.00 • 978-1-933372-93-8

**Carlo Lucarelli**
*Carte Blanche*
"Lucarelli proves that the dark and sinister are better evoked when one opts for unadulterated grit and grime."—*The San Diego Union-Tribune*
128 pp • $14.95 • 978-1-933372-15-0

*The Damned Season*
"De Luca…is a man both pursuing and pursued. And that makes him one of the more interesting figures in crime fiction."
—*The Philadelphia Inquirer*
128 pp • $14.95 • 978-1-933372-27-3

*Via delle Oche*
"Delivers a resolution true to the series' moral relativism."—*Publishers Weekly*
160 pp • $14.95 • 978-1-933372-53-2

**Edna Mazya**
*Love Burns*
"Combines the suspense of a murder mystery with the absurdity of a Woody Allen movie."—*Kirkus*
224 pp • $14.95 • 978-1-933372-08-2

**Sélim Nassib**
*I Loved You for Your Voice*
"Nassib spins a rhapsodic narrative out of the indissoluble connection between two creative souls."—*Kirkus*
272 pp • $14.95 • 978-1-933372-07-5

*The Palestinian Lover*
"A delicate, passionate novel in which history and life are inextricably entwined."
—*RAI Books*
192 pp • $14.95 • 978-1-933372-23-5

**Amélie Nothomb**
*Tokyo Fiancée*
"Intimate and honest…depicts perfectly a nontraditional romance."
—*Publishers Weekly*
160 pp • $15.00 • 978-1-933372-64-8

**Valeria Parrella**
*For Grace Received*
"A voice that is new, original, and decidedly unique."—*Rolling Stone* (Italy)
144 pp • $15.00 • 978-1-933372-94-5